This Attraction Felt So Right, But It Was So Incredibly Wrong.

Jared was her article subject, her employer, one of the most powerful entrepreneurs in Chicago. Melissa had absolutely no business becoming attracted to him.

He reached out to brush a stray lock of hair from her temple. His touch was electric, arousing, light as a feather but shocking as a lightning bolt.

Thunder rumbled in the distance, and the first fat raindrops clattered on the roof.

"I'm going to kiss you," he told her.

She drew a sharp breath. "You think that's a good idea?"

He moved slightly closer. "It's not the smartest thing I've ever done. But I've never wanted anything more."

Dear Reader,

Welcome to book number one in the MONTANA
MILLIONAIRES: THE RYDERS series from the
Silhouette Desire line. I love writing about siblings,
and I hope you enjoy reading Jared's story in
Seduction and the CEO, along with his brother Royce's
and his sister Stephanie's stories over the next couple of
months.

The idea for this series goes back a long time. When I
was ten years old my parents took me to visit my aunt
and uncle's ranch during the summer break from school.
Even at that young age, I spun fanciful stories about the
people living and working on the cattle ranch. I thought
the cowboys were exotic and exciting, and I loved the
space and isolation that gave such a sense of community.

Montana is one of my favorite states and—since the
source for my hero is my husband, a pilot, a cowboy and
a business owner all rolled into one—the stories came
together naturally.

Happy reading!

Barbara

BARBARA DUNLOP

SEDUCTION AND THE CEO

Published by Silhouette Books

America's Publisher of Contemporary Romance

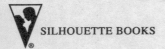

SILHOUETTE BOOKS

ISBN-13: 978-0-373-73009-4

Recycling programs for this product may not exist in your area.

SEDUCTION AND THE CEO

Visit Silhouette Books at www.eHarlequin.com

Printed in U.S.A.

Books by Barbara Dunlop

Silhouette Desire

Thunderbolt over Texas #1704
Marriage Terms #1741
The Billionaire's Bidding #1793
The Billionaire Who Bought Christmas #1836
Beauty and the Billionaire #1853
Marriage, Manhattan Style #1897
Transformed Into the Frenchman's Mistress #1929
*Seduction and the CEO #1996

*Montana Millionaires: The Ryders

BARBARA DUNLOP

writes romantic stories while curled up in a log cabin in Canada's far north, where bears outnumber people and it snows six months of the year. Fortunately, she has a brawny husband and two teenage children to haul firewood and clear the driveway while she sips cocoa and muses about her upcoming chapters. Barbara loves to hear from readers. You can contact her through her Web site at www.barbaradunlop.com.

For my amazing husband—
cowboy, pilot and businessman.

One

Journalist Brandon Langard's blunder was the talk of the bullpen at *Windy City Bizz*. The odds-on favorite for a promotion to feature writer, he'd struck out in his attempt to get an interview with Jared Ryder.

Melissa Warner and the rest of the sixth-floor magazine staff watched the fallout with morbid fascination. The managing editor's door was closed tight, but through the interior window, it was obvious Seth Strickland was shouting. His eyes snapped fire, and his face had turned a mottled purple. Brandon's head was bent and still, his shoulders hunched.

"They've already designed the cover," photographer Susan Alaric stage-whispered over the low barrier between her and Melissa's desks.

"That's because Brandon swore it was a done deal,"

said Melissa, remembering his swagger last week when he'd announced the plum assignment.

"Nothing wrong with that man's confidence," Susan returned with an eye roll. Brandon's habit of bragging, flirting and ogling the female staff had long since alienated them.

"I was sure he'd pull it off," Melissa had to admit. Brandon might be obnoxious, but he was also driven and hardworking. And like all the journalists at the *Bizz,* he knew an in-depth article on Chicago's most elusive entrepreneur and bachelor would clinch the promotion to feature writer.

That Jared Ryder had made a fortune in the Chicago real estate market fit *Windy City Bizz*'s mandate for business news. That he was the heartthrob of half the city's female population suited the magazine's new focus on circulation numbers.

Seth became even more animated, gesticulating with both arms as he rounded his cluttered desk to confront Brandon face-to-face. The occasional word filtered through the closed door. "…incompetent…unreliable… reckless…"

"Ouch." Susan cringed.

Melissa experienced a fleeting twinge of pity for Brandon. But then she remembered how he'd eavesdropped on her conversation with the Women in Business organization last month and presented the story idea as his own. She still owed him for that one. Or rather, he still owed her.

She paused on that thought.

It was true. He *did* owe her one. And maybe it was time to collect.

It would serve him right if she swooped in on this particular story. And why not? Seth clearly needed the Jared Ryder interview. And Melissa would kill for a chance at that promotion.

Through the window, Seth stopped talking. His breathing went deep, his nostrils flared, as he set his jaw in a grim line. Brandon bolted for the office door, and Melissa saw her chance. She quickly came to her feet.

Susan glanced up quizzically, assessing the determined expression on Melissa's face. She obviously came to the right conclusion.

"Do it," she begged with a grin. "Oh, *please* do it."

Melissa's heart upped its rhythm. She swallowed hard, trying not to think about the career-limiting consequences of failure. If she promised the interview and didn't deliver, she'd be in more trouble than Brandon.

Still, as Brandon yanked Seth's door open, she tamped down her fear and made her move.

Her colleagues' gazes hit her from all sides as she made a beeline for the editor's office. Some probably guessed her plan. Others would be simply shocked to see her approaching Seth before he had a chance to calm down. His tirades were legendary. They normally sent the staff scurrying for cover.

Brandon peeled off to the right, studiously avoiding eye contact with anyone.

Melissa rapped on the still-open door. "Seth?"

"What?" he barked, without looking up, rustling through a pile of papers on his cluttered desk.

She took a couple of steps into the office, clicking the door shut behind her.

His round face was flushed all the way to his receding hairline. There was a sheen of sweat above his bushy brows. His white shirt was rumpled, sleeves rolled up. And his tie was loose and dangling in two sections over his protruding belly.

"I can get you the interview," she stated outright, standing tall, her three-inch pumps giving her a slight height advantage.

"What interview?"

"The Jared Ryder interview."

"No. You can't."

"I can," she insisted, voice firm with the confidence she'd learned facing down five older brothers. "I will. What's the deadline?"

"Ryder left Chicago this morning."

"No problem. Where'd he go?"

Seth glared at her without answering.

"I can do it, Seth."

"He turned Langard down flat."

"I'm not Langard."

"You're not," Seth agreed in a tone that told her she'd never be as good as Brandon Langard. Then he picked up his phone and punched in a number.

"Give me a chance," Melissa insisted, closing the space between the door and his desk. "What can it hurt?"

"We're out of time."

"A week," said Melissa. "Give me a week."

"Is Everett available?" Seth asked into the phone.

Everett was publisher of the *Bizz,* the head honcho, the guy who approved the lead headlines and the cover copy.

"Can we at least talk about it?" she pressed.

"Nothing to talk about. Ryder ran off to Montana."

That information took Melissa by surprise. "What's Jared Ryder doing in Montana?" Surely he wasn't building a skyscraper in Butte.

"He's holed up at his ranch."

Melissa hadn't known he had a ranch. Sure, there were rumors he was once a cowboy. But there were also rumors he was once a spy.

Seth gauged her confused look and raised his bushy brows. "You didn't know he had a ranch."

She couldn't argue that one.

"It's the foundation of the entire Ryder conglomerate. How're you going to save my ass when you didn't even know he had a ranch?"

"Because I will," said Melissa with determination. Just because she didn't happen to know Jared was a cowboy didn't mean she couldn't get an interview. "I'll fly to Montana."

"He hates the press. He really hates the *Bizz.* He'll probably run you off his land with—" Seth's attention went to the telephone. "Everett?"

"I can do it," Melissa said, feeling her big chance slip away.

"I have a situation," Seth said to Everett.

"I'll get on the ranch," she pressed in an undertone,

her mind scrambling. "I'll go undercover. I *will* get you the story."

Seth's attention never left the telephone. "It's the Jared Ryder interview." He paused, face flushing deeper, while Everett obviously voiced his displeasure.

"Have I ever let you down?" Melissa went on. She hadn't. But then, she'd never tackled anything this big, either.

"Yes. I know I did," Seth said to Everett.

"Please," said Melissa, leaning forward. "I'll buy my own plane ticket."

Seth shoulders tensed. "Langard *was* the best I—"

While Everett obviously weighed in again, Melissa searched her mind for fresh arguments.

"I grew up with horses," she blurted out. Well, one horse, really. It had lived in a field, on the edge of suburbia, across the street from her new house. She'd nicknamed it Midnight. "I'll—"

Seth's glare warned her to shut up.

"—get a job on the ranch."

Seth smacked his palm over the mouthpiece. "Do you know who this is?"

She gave a small nod.

"Get out."

"But—"

"Now."

Melissa pursed her lips.

Seth's gaze glittered dark with warning as he went back to Everett. "The Cooper story can take the cover."

Melissa debated a split second longer. But bravery

was one thing, stupidity quite another. She'd pushed Seth as far as she dared.

She retreated, and Seth's voice followed her back to the bullpen. "I'll get a photographer on it right away."

Like Brandon had done only minutes before, she avoided eye contact as she made her way to her desk.

"Susan," Seth bellowed from behind her.

With a darting look of pity at Melissa, Susan rolled back her chair, came to her feet and headed for the editor's office.

Melissa dropped into her own chair and stared at the randomly bouncing colored balls of her screen saver. She could have gotten that interview. She knew she could have gotten that interview.

"It's Lorne Cooper on the cover," said Susan as she slipped back into her seat.

Melissa nodded with resignation. "The sports-gear king." There was a new megastore opening on Murdoch Street, and "Cruisin' Cooper" was sponsoring a bicycle race to celebrate.

"The article's written. All it needs is an update and some new art."

Melissa pulled herself closer to her computer screen and hit the space bar. "It was written by R. J. Holmes," she pointed out, voice laced with self-pity. R.J. was one of the newest journalists on staff, and he was beating her out for a cover.

"I guess Seth wasn't feeling charitable toward Brandon."

"Or toward me." Melissa's screen powered up on a search engine.

"What've you got ready?"

"Myers Corp. or the Briggs' merger."

Susan didn't answer.

"I know," Melissa conceded, randomly poking the *H* key. "They're even lamer than Cooper." Not that any old cover story would clinch the promotion. There was only one story that would catapult her into the feature writer's job.

She backspaced to erase the *H* and typed Jared Ryder into the search engine.

In a split second, it returned a list of options that included the home page of Ryder International, Jared's speech last month to the Chamber of Commerce, contact information for his new office tower and a link to the Ryder Ranch.

Curious, she clicked the ranch link.

A brilliant green panorama of trees, meadows and rolling hills appeared in front of her. The sky was crackling turquoise, while a ribbon of pale blue meandered through the meadow, nearly kissing a two-story, red-roofed house surrounded by pens and outbuildings.

So that was what Montana looked like.

A row of thumbnail pictures lined the bottom of the screen. "Natural beauty," advertised one caption. "Surrounded by wilderness," read another. "South of Glacier National Park."

Susan shut down her own computer, rising to sling three cameras over her shoulder. "Gotta get to work."

"Have fun," Melissa offered, clicking on a thumbnail

of summer wildflowers. Red, purple, yellow, white. They really were quite gorgeous.

Susan grinned as she pushed a drawer shut with her hip. "I will. Headshots today. Then there's a gala Friday night, and I'm going to hitch a ride on the channel-ten chopper for the bike race Sunday."

"Shut up," Melissa griped as Susan rounded the end of the desk.

Melissa would be sitting right here all week long, in the stuffy, hot office, combing through the minutes of various City Hall committees, looking for permits or variances or financial-policy news, anything that might lead to an interesting business story.

"What's that?" asked Susan, nodding to the computer screen.

Melissa refocused on the verdant green and bright flowers. "Montana," she answered. "Where *I'd* be if Seth had half a heart." *Or half a brain.*

She clicked on an area map. There was an airport in Missoula and everything.

"Not my cup of tea," said Susan, popping a jaunty plaid hat on her curly brown locks.

"Not mine, either," Melissa admitted, gathering her own straight, blond hair into a knot at the nape of her neck in an effort to let the building's weak air-conditioning waft over her hot skin. "But I'd fly there in a heartbeat to meet Jared Ryder."

"So do it," said Susan.

"Yeah, right."

"Why not?"

Melissa swiveled to face her coworker. "Because Seth turned me down flat."

Susan shrugged. "Tell him you're doing City Hall research from home. Then get on a plane."

Oh, now that seemed brilliant. "Lie to my boss and ignore his orders?"

"He'll forgive you if you get the story." Susan's lips curved in a conspiratorial grin. "Trust me."

Melissa let the hair slip out of her hand. The idea was preposterous.

Susan leaned in and lowered her voice. "If you don't get the story, somebody else will."

"At least it won't be Brandon."

"Result will be the same."

"Flying to Montana could get me fired," Melissa pointed out.

"It could also get you promoted." Susan straightened.

"Easy for you to say."

Susan shrugged the cameras into a more comfortable position, then adjusted her cap. "Up to you. But no risk, no reward. My biggest payday was when those vandals let the lions loose at Lincoln Park."

"That was insane," Melissa reminded her. Susan had been clinging to the branches of an oak tree with a hungry male lion pacing below when the animal-control officer had darted the thing.

Another shrug.

"Are you suggesting that if I don't put myself in mortal danger, I'm not trying hard enough?"

Susan patted Melissa's shoulder. "I'm suggesting if

you don't torpedo Brandon and go after that promotion, you're not trying hard enough."

Point made, Susan winked and sauntered away, while Melissa drummed her fingertips on the desktop.

She glanced at the pictures of the Montana ranch. Then her gaze shifted to the spacious window cubicle reserved for the new feature writer.

She pictured Seth's expression when she presented the article. She pictured Brandon's face when he learned of her coup. She pictured her byline on the cover of the *Bizz.* Then just for good measure, she pictured herself at the podium, accepting a Prentice award next January. She could wear her black-and-gold-layered gown, with the teardrop medallion she'd found last week in that funky little art gallery on Second.

Take *that,* Brandon Langard.

Her life would be perfect. All she had to do was talk her way onto the Ryder Ranch.

Body loose in the saddle, Jared Ryder held his horse Tango to a slow walk across the wooden bridge that led to his sister Stephanie's place. Her jumping-horse outfit was built on Ryder land up on the Bonaparte Plateau, about ten miles into the hills from the main spread at Spirit Lake. Tango's ears twitched and his body tensed as he took in the nearly hundred head of horses grazing in the fields and milling about in the pens clustered around the main riding arena.

Jared was feeling just as twitchy as his horse. Far from the haven he'd always known, the familiar sights

and sounds of Montana brought a crush of memories.
And a fresh surge of anger roiled in his belly.

His instinct had been to stay far away from the ranch
this week. But his sister, Stephanie, needed him. Besides,
Chicago had its own problems at the moment.

Ryder International had just signed a long-term lease
to rent space to the City of Chicago in the Ryder office
tower that was under construction on Washington Street.
For some reason, the mayor had insisted on parading
Jared from charity ball to art gallery opening. Jared had
been out in public so often that the tabloids started to
believe there was a reason to take his picture and stuff
a microphone in his face.

It was beyond frustrating. He was a businessman, not
a politician or a celebrity. And his personal life was none
of their damn business. The reporter from *Windy City
Bizz* camping out at the end of his driveway Monday
night was the last straw. When he got back to the city,
he was looking into restraining orders and disguises.

But for the moment he had no choice but to come
to terms with the home front. He cleared the main
equestrian barn, and a cluster of people on horseback at
the riding arena came into view. His appearance caught
their attention. One horse and rider immediately broke
free from the group, trotting down the dirt road to meet
him. Both Jared and Tango tracked the pair's progress
past the pens, dotted outbuildings and sparse trees.

"The prodigal returns," sang his twenty-two-year-old
sister, Stephanie, pulling her mare to a halt, raising a
cloud of dust in the July sunshine. Her smiling, freckle-
flecked face peeked out from her riding helmet. Her long

legs were clad in tight jodhpurs and high, glossy brown boots, while a loose, tan blouse ballooned around her small frame. Her unruly auburn hair was tied back in a ponytail.

"I think you're confusing me with Royce," said Jared, watching her closely. She might not know what he knew, but they'd all been shaken by their grandfather's death three months ago.

He halted Tango, who eyed the mare with suspicion.

"At least Royce makes it to my competitions," Stephanie pointed out, shifting in her stirrups. "He was there to watch me win last week at Spruce Meadows."

"That's because he lives on his jet plane," Jared defended. His brother, Royce, routinely flew from New York to London, Rome and points east, checking out companies to add to the Ryder International empire. Royce was mobile.

"I live in a boardroom," Jared finished.

"Poor baby," Stephanie teased. She smiled, but Jared caught the veiled sadness in her silver-blue eyes. Stephanie had been only two when their parents died, and Gramps was the closest thing to a parent she'd known.

"Congratulations," he told her softly, reflexively tamping down his own anger to focus on her needs. He'd been fifteen when they lost their parents, and he liked to think he'd had a hand in raising her, too. He was immensely proud of her accomplishments as both a rider and a trainer.

"Thanks." She leaned forward to pat Rosie-Jo, her

champion gray Hanoverian, briskly on the neck, but not before Jared caught the telltale sheen in her eyes. "Want to see our trophy?"

"Of course," he answered. There would be plenty of time later to talk about their grandfather.

"We've got a few hours before the meeting." She drew a brave breath and squared her shoulders, shaking off the sadness as she turned the horse to draw alongside Jared.

Together they headed toward her two-story blue-gabled ranch house.

The annual meeting of the Genevieve Memorial Fund, a charitable trust named in memory of their mother, would take place today. Each year, it was scheduled to coincide with the anniversary of their parents' deaths. Picturing his parents, Jared felt his anger percolating once more. But he had to suck it up, be a man about it. There was absolutely no point in disillusioning his younger brother and sister.

"I saw *you* in the Chicago paper last week," Stephanie chimed in as they left the river behind them.

"That was a picture of the mayor," Jared corrected. He'd done his best to duck behind the burly man.

"They named you in the caption."

"Slow news day," he told her, remembering the flashbulbs outside the gallery and how the reporters had shouted inane questions as he'd helped Nadine into the limo.

Stephanie's expression turned calculating, her tone curious. "So who was she?"

"Who was who?" he asked, pretending he didn't

know exactly where his baby sister was headed. Raised in a male-dominated household, she'd been lobbying for *somebody* to please marry a nice woman since she was seven years old.

"The bombshell in the picture with you."

"She was my date," he offered, letting the statement dangle without elaboration.

Stephanie pasted him with a look of impatience. "And?"

He forced her to wait a beat longer. "And her name is Nadine Romsey. Sorry to disappoint you, but she's not a bombshell. She's a lawyer with Comcoe Newsome."

Stephanie's interest grew. "Looks *and* brains. This must be something serious."

"It was a business arrangement. The mayor invited me to the party, and there were people attending that Nadine wanted to meet."

Stephanie pouted. "But she's so pretty."

"And you're so hopelessly romantic."

"Will you take her out again?"

"Only if she needs to get into another party." He admired Nadine, but he didn't have any romantic interest in her.

Stephanie compressed her lips in frustration. "You've written her off after one date? You know, you're never going to meet a woman if you don't get out there and—"

"I'm 'out there' 24/7, little sister." He gestured around the spread. "That's what pays for all of this."

Stephanie pointed her nose in the air. "Ryder

Equestrian Center brought in a million dollars last year."

Jared snorted a laugh. "While you spent four million."

"We also provided dozens of marketing opportunities for the firm, and we improved your corporate image. That is priceless."

"You rehearsed that, didn't you?"

"You should get married, Jared."

"Aren't you a little old to be angling for a mother figure?"

"I'm looking for a sister now. You should find someone young and fun. Who likes horses," she added for good measure, kicking her mare into a faster walk.

Jared shook his head. Between the revelation his grandfather had spoken on his deathbed, the mayor and the media, and Ryder International's accountant's concerns that the company was expanding too fast, Jared didn't have a scrap of emotional or intellectual energy left over for romance.

As he followed Stephanie past the open door of a stable, a sudden tingle spread up his spine. He turned sharply and locked gazes with a blond-haired, green-eyed beauty who stood just inside the main doorway. She was wearing blue jeans and a crisp white shirt, and she held a manure fork in both hands.

She quickly glanced away, but his radar pinged.

What was it?

He stared at her a little longer.

It was the makeup. Her makeup was subtle, but she was definitely wearing some. And he'd bet her blond highlights were from a salon, not the sunshine. Her collared shirt was pressed, and the hands that held the manure fork were soft, bare, no gloves.

"Who's that?" he asked his sister.

Stephanie turned and followed the direction of his gaze.

"Why? You think she's pretty?"

Anyone could see the woman was gorgeous. But that wasn't the point.

"I think she's a rank greenhorn," he said.

"Her name's Melissa…something. Webster, I think. You want me to introduce you?" The calculating flare was back in Stephanie's eyes.

"Stop," Jared ordered.

His sister grinned unrepentantly.

"What I want you to do," he continued with exaggerated patience, "is to hire experienced staff. We're blowing enough money on this place as it is."

"She needed a job," said Stephanie. "She's from Indiana."

He wasn't sure what the hell Indiana had to do with anything. While he watched, the woman awkwardly scooped a pile of horse manure from the wooden floor and dumped it into a wheelbarrow. "If she needed a million dollars, would you give it to her?"

"She didn't ask for a million dollars. She's on her way to Seattle. She needed money for bus fare."

"You're hiring transients now?"

"She's mucking out our stalls, Jared, not signing the company checks."

"I'm not worried about embezzlement. I'm worried about labor cost efficiency."

He was also worried something wasn't quite right. Why would a woman that polished take a menial job for bus fare?

She could be running away from something, he supposed. Or she could be running from some*one*. Which seemed more likely. An ex-boyfriend? Someone's angry wife? It had better not be the FBI or the state troopers.

He considered her delicate profile, trying to decide if she was a criminal. She tackled the next pile of manure, her city-soft hands sliding up and down the wooden handle.

"She's going to get blisters," he voiced the thought out loud.

"You want to give her some gloves?" asked Stephanie.

"Somebody better," he conceded. Aimless wanderer or criminal on the run, if they were going to employ her, the least they could do was make sure she avoided injury.

"Hey, Melissa," Stephanie called.

The woman paused and glanced up.

"Grab some gloves out of the storeroom."

Melissa gave her hands a puzzled look.

"She hasn't a clue," said Jared, hit with an unexpected flash of pity. Maybe she was running from an angry ex. He quickly reined in his thoughts. None of his business.

"You *sure* you don't want me to introduce you?" Stephanie singsonged.

Jared turned Tango toward the house. "You going to show me your trophy or what?"

"Can't blame a girl for trying."

"Yes, I can." But Jared glanced over his shoulder one last time as they moved away. Manure fork balanced in the crook of her elbow, the woman named Melissa was wriggling her fingers into the pair of stiff leather gloves. The fork slipped and banged to the wooden floor. The sound startled a horse. The horse startled the woman. She tripped on the fork and landed with a thud on her backside.

Their gazes met once more, his amused, hers annoyed.

He turned away, but the flash of emerald stayed with him as he followed Stephanie to the hitching rail in front of the house.

Two

By the end of the day, the bruise on Melissa's left butt cheek had settled to a dull ache.

While she swept the last of the straw from the stable floor, a late-model Bentley rumbled its way to the front of the farmhouse. The glossy black exterior might be dusty, but it was still one impressive automobile. And the chauffeur who jumped out of the driver's seat was crisp in his uniform.

She moved into the oversize doorway, leaning on the end of the broom handle while she waited to see who would emerge from the backseat.

It was an older man, distinguished in a Savile Row suit. He was tall, with a head of thick silver hair. He nodded politely to the chauffeur, then headed up the stairs to the wraparound porch, where both Stephanie and Jared appeared to greet him and usher him inside.

The chauffeur shut the car door. He glanced curiously around the ranch yard before moving to open the trunk. Melissa peered at the house, but there was no way to guess what was going on inside. The man might be a friend, or perhaps he was a business associate.

Jared's sister's house seemed like an odd location for a business meeting. Unless, of course, somebody wanted to keep the meeting a secret.

Now *that* was an interesting possibility. Was there something clandestine in the works for Ryder International?

As the chauffeur had before her, Melissa glanced curiously around the yard. Several young riders were practicing jumps in the main ring, their grooms and trainers watching. A group of stable hands were loading hay into a pickup truck beside the biggest barn, and three cowboys were urging a small herd of horses across the river with a pair of border collies lending a hand. Nobody was paying the slightest bit of attention to the Bentley.

Then another vehicle appeared and pulled up to the house. This one was an SUV, larger but no less luxurious than the Bentley.

A thirtysomething man with dark glasses and curly dark hair stepped out of the driver's seat. He looked Mediterranean, and he was definitely not a chauffeur. He wore loafers, well-cut blue jeans, an open white dress shirt and a dark jacket. He also offered a polite greeting to the Bentley driver before striding up the stairs of the porch.

Melissa's journalistic curiosity all but ordered her to investigate. She leaned her broom up against the stable wall and started across the yard. She told herself she'd put in a good eight hours today. It was close to dinnertime, and the Bentley was at least vaguely in the direction of the cookhouse. She'd have a plausible excuse if anyone questioned her.

Ironically she'd been disappointed not to get a job down at the main ranch. The foreman there had all but sent her packing this morning when she'd told him she was a stranded traveler. Luckily Stephanie Ryder had been there at the time. The younger woman had taken pity on Melissa and offered her a job at the Ryder Equestrian Center. Melissa had been plotting ways to get back to the main ranch when Jared and his horse had wandered into the yard. Talk about good luck.

Now she was looking for more luck. She smiled brightly at the chauffeur, smudging her palms along the sides of her thighs, wishing she wasn't covered in dust and sweat, and was wearing something other than blue jeans and a grime-streaked shirt. She wasn't the greatest flirt in the world, but in the right party dress, she could usually hold a man's attention.

"Very nice car," she ventured in a friendly voice as she approached.

The man pushed the trunk closed and gazed critically at the Bentley. "I suppose dust is better than mud."

She guessed he was about her own age, maybe twenty-five or twenty-six. He was attractive, in a farmboyfresh kind of way, with blond hair, a straight nose and a narrow chin. He was clean-shaven, and his hair was neatly trimmed.

She slowed her steps, taking in the Montana license plate and committing the number to memory. "Did you have a long drive in?" she asked pleasantly.

"Couple of hours from Helena."

Helena. Good. That was a start. "So you work in Helena?"

"Three years now."

She stayed silent for a moment, hoping he'd elaborate on his job or the company. She scanned both his uniform and the car for a logo.

"Your first time at Ryder Ranch?" She tried another approach.

He nodded at that. "Heard about it, of course. Everybody in the state knows about the Ryders."

"I'm from Indiana," she supplied.

"Grew up south of Butte myself." He gave the dust on the car another critical gaze. "There a hose around here someplace?"

She had no idea. "I guess you meet interesting people in your job?" She struggled to keep the conversation focused on his employment.

"I do some." He glanced around the ranch yard while a horse whinnied in the distance, and a tractor engine roared to life. Unfortunately he didn't pick up the conversational thread.

But Melissa wasn't giving up, not by a long shot. She moved in a step closer, tossing back her hair, hoping it looked disheveled, instead of unruly.

Her actions caught his attention, and he glanced at the ground.

She lowered her voice as she gave him her brightest smile. "I'm a little embarrassed," she cooed. "But should I know the man you dropped off?"

The chauffeur looked back up. He didn't answer. Instead, he swallowed hard, and his neck flushed beneath the collar of his uniform.

"I only ask," she continued, tilting her head to one side, surprised it took so little to rattle him, "because I don't want…"

He worked his jaw.

She paused, waiting for him, but he didn't make a sound.

She suddenly realized his gaze wasn't fixed on her. He was focused on a spot behind her left shoulder. Her scalp prickled.

Uh-oh. She twisted her head and came face-to-face with Jared Ryder.

It was clear he was annoyed. He was also taller than she'd realized, and intimidating, with that strong chin and those deep blue eyes. He wore a fitted, Western-cut shirt and snug blue jeans. His shoulders were broad, his chest deep, and his sleeves were rolled halfway up his forearms, revealing a deep tan and obvious muscle definition.

"Don't want to what?" he asked Melissa, his tone a low rumbling challenge.

She didn't have a quick answer for that, and his deep blue gaze flicked to the silent chauffeur. "There's coffee in the cookhouse." He gave the man a nod in the appropriate direction.

The chauffeur immediately took his cue and hustled away.

Jared's tone turned to steel, the power of his irritation settling fully on Melissa. "I'd sure appreciate it if you could flirt on your own time."

"I…" What could she tell him? That she wasn't flirting? That, in fact, she was spying?

Better to go with flirting.

"I'm sorry," she told him, offering no excuses.

He gave a curt nod of acknowledgment, followed by a long assessing gaze that made her glad she was only pretending to be his employee.

"I don't know why Stephanie hired you," he finally stated.

Melissa wasn't sure how to answer that, or even if he expected an answer. The only thing she did know was that she was determined to take advantage of the opportunity to talk to him alone.

"You're Stephanie's brother?" she asked, pretending she hadn't been poring over his press coverage on the Internet.

"She tells me you grew up around horses," he countered, instead of answering the question.

"I did." Melissa nodded. Technically it was true. She gestured to the northern paddocks. "You obviously grew up around a lot of them."

"My qualifications aren't at issue."

"Stephanie seemed fine with mine." Melissa valiantly battled the nerves bubbling in her stomach. "I saw the main house yesterday. The one your grandparents built. Were you born on the Ryder Ranch?"

A muscle ticked in his left cheek. "Since you're obviously not busy with anything else, I need you to move my horse to the riverside pen. The one with the red gate."

"Sure." The brave word jumped out before she had a chance to censor it.

"Name's Tango." Jared pointed to a paddock on the other side of the driveway turnaround where a black horse pranced and bucked his way around the fence line. Its head was up, ears pointed, and it was tossing his mane proudly for the three horses in the neighboring pen.

Melissa's bravado instantly evaporated.

"You can tack him up if you like," Jared continued. "Or he's fine bareback."

Bareback? She swallowed. Not that a saddle would help.

"Melissa?"

Okay. New plan. Forget the interview, it was time for a quick exit.

"I…just…" she stammered. "I…uh…just remembered, I'm off shift."

His brows twitched upward. "We have shifts?"

"I mean…" She blinked up at him. What? *What?* What the hell did she say?

She rubbed the bruise on her left butt cheek, making a show of wincing. "My fall. Earlier. I'm a little stiff and sore."

"Too stiff to sit on a horse?" He clearly found the excuse preposterous.

"I'm also a little rusty." She attempted to look contrite and embarrassed. "I haven't ridden for a while."

He cocked his head, studying her all over again. "It's like riding a bike."

She was sure it was.

"Tack's on the third stand. Don't let him hold his breath when you cinch the saddle."

As far as she was concerned, Tango could do any old thing he pleased. She wasn't going to stop him from holding his breath. Quite frankly she'd rather chase lions around Lincoln Park.

"I really can't—"

"We fire people who can't get the job done," Jared flatly warned her.

The threat stopped Melissa cold. If she got fired, she'd be thrown off the property. She could kiss the article and her promotion goodbye. And if Seth found out she'd been here, she could probably kiss her job at the *Bizz* goodbye, too.

"I hope you won't," she said in all sincerity.

Jared searched her expression for a long moment. His voice went low, and the space between them grew smaller. "Give me one reason why I shouldn't."

"I've been working really hard," she told him without hesitation.

"Not at the moment," he pointed out.

"It's six o'clock."

"We're not nine to five on Ryder Ranch."

"I'm prepared for that."

He edged almost imperceptibly closer, revealing tiny laugh lines beside his eyes and a slight growth of beard along his tanned square jaw. "Are you?"

She ignored the tug of attraction to his rugged masculinity. "Yes."

"You'll pull your own weight?"

"I will."

"You can't depend on your looks around here."

Melissa drew back in surprise.

"If I catch you batting those big green eyes—"

"I never—"

He leaned closer still and she shut her mouth. "You mess with my cowboys, and your pretty little butt will be off the property in a heartbeat."

A rush of heat prickled her cheeks. "I have *no* intention of messing with your cowboys."

A cloud rolled over the setting sun, and a chill dampened the charged air between them.

Jared's nostrils flared, and his eyes darkened to indigo in the shifting light. He stared at her for a lengthening moment, then his head canted to one side.

How his kiss might feel bloomed unbidden in her mind. It would be light, then firm, then harder still as he pulled her body flush against his own. A flash of heat stirred her body as the wind gusted between them, forming tiny dust devils on the driveway and rustling the tall, summer grass.

The ranch hands still shouted to one another. Hooves still thudded against the packed dirt. And the diesel engines still rumbled in the distance.

"See that you don't," he finally murmured. "And move my damn horse."

"Fine," she ground out, quashing the stupid hormonal reaction. She'd move the damn horse or die trying.

Later that evening, in Stephanie's dining room, Jared struggled to put Melissa out of his mind. His sister had obviously hired the woman out of pity. Then Jared had kept her on for the same reason. He wasn't sure who'd made the bigger mistake.

"We've had thirty-five new requests for assistance this year," said Otto Durand, moving a manila file to the top of his pile. Otto had been a board member of the Genevieve Memorial Fund for fifteen years. He was also the CEO of Rutledge Agricultural Equipment and a lifelong friend of Jared and Melissa's parents.

"We do have the money," Anthony Salvatore put in, flipping through a report. "Donations, they are up nearly twenty percent." Anthony was a distant relative, the son of Jared's mother's cousin. The cousin had met and fallen in love with Carmine Salvatore on a college trip to Naples, and their only son had held a special place in Genevieve's heart.

Stephanie replaced the empty bottle of merlot on the large oblong table as the housekeeper cleared away the last of the dinner dishes.

Although Royce was stuck in London until Saturday, the remaining four board members of the Genevieve Fund were empowered to make decisions on this year's projects.

"I like the school in West Africa," said Stephanie.

"Most of the kids in that region are from agricultural families."

"Mom would like that," Jared acknowledged, then caught Stephanie's fleeting wince. This year in particular, he knew his sister felt a hole in her life where her mother should have been.

Along with their grandfather, he and Royce had struggled to keep their mother's memory alive for her, showing videos, telling stories, displaying mementos. But there was a loneliness inside her that they couldn't seem to fill. It had always manifested itself in hard work and a driving need to succeed. Jared only had to look at the row of equestrian jumping trophies along the mantelpiece to know how hard she pushed herself.

"Yes to the West Africa school." Otto put a check mark on page three of his report. "And I think we can all agree on increasing the animal shelter contributions. Now, the South American clinic project?"

"I still think it's too dangerous," said Jared. He knew his brother, Royce, had advocated for the project after meeting a British university student who'd worked in the mountainous region. But there were too many unknowns, too many frightening stories coming out of the area.

"The rebel activity has been down in that area for six months now," Anthony put in. "And we will use a contractor with experience in the area."

"What about security?" Jared countered. It wasn't the first time the Genevieve Fund had worked in an unstable part of the world, but the other projects had a multiagency, multinational presence, and security had been provided by experts.

"We will hire our own security," said Anthony.

Jared wasn't going to be easily convinced. "For the cost of private security, we could take on two other projects."

"None that are as critical as this one," said Anthony, warming up to the debate. The two of them settled into a familiar rhythm of point counterpoint, each trying to convince Stephanie and Otto of the merits of their respective positions.

Jared acknowledged it was a worthwhile project, while Anthony acknowledged the security circumstances were less than ideal. Still, on balance, Jared felt the situation was far too dangerous, and he made that clear in no uncertain terms.

Finally Anthony threw up his hands in frustration. "I am going for some air."

Fine with Jared. It would give him a few minutes alone with Stephanie and Otto to solidify his case.

Stephanie stood to stretch, while Otto dropped his pen on the report in front of him, speaking before Jared had a chance. "Maybe we should go with Anthony and Royce on this one."

"And if somebody gets kidnapped or killed?" It was a worst-case scenario, but it was also a realistic one.

"They have signed a ceasefire," Otto said.

"Not worth the paper it's printed on. It's Sierra Benito, for goodness' sake. The political situation could turn on a dime." Jared's gaze caught Anthony's profile through the gauzy curtains.

"How many kidnappings last year?" asked Stephanie.

"Too many," replied Jared.

"Nothing since December," said Otto. "I don't want to go against you on—"

"And I'm not looking for risk-free," Jared stressed. "And I don't mind spending the extra money on security. But do we *really* want to take Royce's advice on what's dangerous and what's not?"

Neither Otto nor Stephanie had an answer for that.

In the sudden silence Jared caught another movement on the porch. But this time it wasn't Anthony's profile. It was...

"Excuse me for a moment." He rose from his chair, ignoring their looks of surprise as he crossed to the front door.

"We still have the family home in Naples," Anthony was saying to Melissa as Jared pushed open the screen door. "And I visit it as often as possible." Anthony had planted his butt against the log railing of the porch, one arm bracing him on each side while Melissa stood in front of him.

"I've always wanted to see Italy." She sighed. "The Colosseum, Vatican City, the Sistine Chapel."

Jared scoffed. Pretty big dreams for a woman who couldn't even make it to Seattle.

Anthony levered himself forward to standing, and Melissa didn't back off.

"I would love to show you Venice," he said in a voice that promised more than a tour of the Grand Canal.

Jared wasn't sure who he should warn—Melissa that

Anthony was a player, or Anthony that Melissa's only life skill appeared to be flirting.

"I assume you moved my horse?" he said, instead, causing her to turn her head. Once again she looked both guilty and surprised to see him. And once again he was stabbed in the solar plexus with a shot of unwelcome attraction.

He determinedly shook it off.

"Melissa and I were discussing the treasures of Italy," Anthony offered conversationally, but the set of his shoulders and the tightness around his mouth told Jared that he didn't welcome the interruption.

Too bad.

"You're supposed to be thinking about Sierra Benito," Jared reminded him, moving through the beam of the porch light, transmitting his clear intention to join the conversation.

"Business can wait," said Anthony.

Jared made a show of glancing at his watch. "It's been a long meeting already."

"Give me five minutes. I will be right in."

But Jared had absolutely no intention of leaving.

Melissa glanced back and forth between the two men. Her expression hadn't changed, but the interest in her eyes was obvious.

"Since Melissa's here—" Jared angled his body toward her "—maybe she has something to contribute. What do you think? Is Sierra Benito too dangerous for a humanitarian project?"

Anthony jumped in. "I am sure Melissa doesn't want to discuss—"

"Do you mean right in Suri City?" she asked. "Or up in the mountains?"

Her answer surprised him. Most people had never heard of Sierra Benito, never mind its capital city.

"A little village called Tappee," he told her.

Her head shook almost imperceptibly, but the small motion emphasized the bounce to her silky blond hair. "Horrible conditions up there. The villagers live in abject poverty."

Anthony chuckled and swung an arm around her shoulders. "I welcome you to the debate, Senorita Melissa."

Jared steeled himself against the urge to rip her out of Anthony's arms. It was a ridiculous reaction. The half hug was a friendly gesture, nothing more.

"Do you have any idea what the gold miners do to the villagers?" Melissa asked. She didn't react to Anthony's hug—didn't lean in, didn't shrug him off, either.

"Do you have any idea what the rebels do to the gold miners?" Jared asked around the clamor of emotion inside his head.

What the hell was the matter with him?

What did he care if Anthony hugged Melissa?

She shook her head in disgust. "I can't believe you're going to exploit them."

Jared jerked back at the accusation. "Exploit *who*?"

"The villagers."

"I'm not going to exploit the villagers." Jared's gaze caught on Anthony's hand and held.

Melissa was wearing a white cotton shirt. It was thin

fabric, hardly a barrier between Anthony's fingertips and her shoulder. Why didn't she shrug him off?

She scoffed. "Right. You'll subcontract the exploitation to Madre Gold to Tomesko Mining."

"That's a leap in logic," he pointed out.

"There's no other reason to go to Tappee."

"We are building a medical clinic," Anthony put in.

"Not necessarily," Jared countered with a warning glare.

Melissa glanced from one to the other with surprise and more than a little curiosity.

"How do you know anything about Tappee?" he couldn't help but probe, watching her closely for signs of…he wasn't even sure what.

"I read the *Chicago Daily*," she answered with a blink, and her green eyes went back to neutral. "There was a story last year about a mining engineer who was kidnapped by rebels."

"The company paid a million dollars." Jared took the story to its conclusion. "And they killed the guy, anyway."

"That was more than a year ago," said Anthony. "And we are not going there to mine."

"You think they care?" asked Jared. "Do you honestly believe they won't take any Westerner hostage?"

"I believe they do care," said Melissa.

"Yeah?" Jared challenged. "Is that conclusion based on your vast travel experience with the American national bus system?"

"Do not be rude," Anthony cut in, anger clear in his tone.

Well, Jared was angry, too. He'd had about enough of the argument, and he'd had about enough of watching Anthony maul Melissa. He grabbed his Stetson hat from a peg on the wall and crammed it on his head.

"I'm going to walk Melissa back to her cottage," he announced, linking her arm and moving her firmly out of Anthony's grasp.

"What in the hell…" Anthony began.

"*You* need to get back to the meeting," Jared ordered over his shoulder, propelling Melissa toward the stairs. It took her a second to get her feet sorted out under her, but he made sure she didn't stumble.

He could feel Anthony watching them as they crossed the darkened yard toward the driveway lights. Jared knew he was going to get an earful back in the house, but he didn't care. He could give just as good as he got.

He marched her forward at a brisk pace. He didn't know which cottage Melissa had been assigned, but single women were usually on the river side of the arena, so he took a chance and turned right.

"Why do I get the feeling this isn't about walking me back to my cabin?" asked Melissa.

Jared gritted his teeth, struggling to bring his emotions back under control. "Why do I get the feeling you're not here to earn money for a bus ticket?"

Three

Melissa ordered herself not to panic. There was no reason to assume he knew the truth. But even as she mentally reassured herself, the roots of her hair prickled in dread.

His pace was brisk, his large hand still wrapped around her upper arm. It felt strong and uncompromising as steel. She wondered if he intended to march her all the way to his property line.

"First the chauffeur." Jared's angry voice cut through the night air. "Then Anthony." He sucked in a tight breath. "And I can guess what went on with the damn horse."

The last took Melissa by surprise.

The *horse?* Why would she interview his horse?

"Ride it yourself?" Jared taunted.

Melissa struggled to make sense out of the accusation. She hadn't ridden the horse herself, but how could that possibly be relevant?

"Or did you get a little help?" he finished on a meaningful lilt.

He obviously already knew she had. There was no point in lying about that. "I got one of the cowboys to help me. Rich or Rand or Rafe…something…"

"I'll just bet you did." The contempt in Jared's voice was crystal clear.

"So what?" Her confusion was starting to turn to annoyance. Rafe had, in fact, offered to help her. The whole operation hadn't taken more than fifteen minutes of his time.

"So *what?*" Jared jerked her to a stop and rounded on her, glaring from beneath his battered tan Stetson.

Melissa caught her breath while she searched his hard expression in the shadowed light. Why was the horse such a salient detail? Shouldn't he be more upset about the way she'd pumped Anthony for information?

Unless…

It suddenly hit her that she'd jumped to the wrong conclusion. She wasn't caught. Jared was angry about her interaction with his cowboys.

"Is there a company ban on cowboys helping stable hands?" she asked.

"No, but I'm thinking about banning *fraternization.*"

His obvious euphemism was more than a little offensive. "You think I had time to *fraternize* with Rafe before dinner?"

Something flickered in his eyes. It might have been regret. "I think flirting is your only life skill."

"It's not." For starters, she had a university degree. She owned real estate. And she had a good job, soon to be a great job if she could pull off this interview.

"Do tell," he challenged.

"I'm intelligent, articulate and organized."

"You couldn't even organize a bus ticket to Seattle."

"Buying the bus ticket ahead of time wasn't the point."

"What was the point?"

"I'm experiencing America."

"By batting your eyes and swaying your hips?"

She held up her blistered palms. "By shoveling your stable for eight hours."

He reached for her wrist, moving her hands under the beam of a yard light, and his expression tightened. "You put something on this?"

"Work gloves." And she wished she'd thought to do it sooner.

"I'm serious."

She pulled her hand from his grasp. "I'm fine."

He took in her body from head to toe. "I don't think you're cut out for manual labor."

She subconsciously shifted her injured hands behind her back. "I told you I was fine."

"You know how to operate a computer? Type? File?"

Oh, no. She wasn't giving up her ranch job. "I've never worked in an office," she lied. "Besides, I only need bus fare. I'll be out of your hair in a week." At least that part was true.

"You might not last a week."

"I lasted a day."

"Maybe." He paused. "But you know those guys you're flirting with are going to eventually expect you to put out."

"No, they won't." She wasn't flirting anywhere near that seriously.

Jared grunted his disbelief.

The man was an alarmist. But he didn't have the worst idea in the world.

Instead of arguing with him, she sidled forward, tucking her hair behind her ears and lowering her voice to a sultry level. "So how far do you think I'll have to go?"

He brows quirked up. "You're flirting with *me?*"

She leaned in. "Is it working?"

He shifted, letting his crooked hip and cocked head transmit his indolence. "All depends on what you're after."

What she wanted was the story of his life. And she was definitely prepared to bat her eyes a little to get it. "An exemption from riding your horse," she said, instead. "He's scary. Where'd you get him?"

"He's a direct descendent of Renegade."

Melissa tilted her head and widened her eyes, letting the silence go on for a moment.

"My great-great-grandfather's stallion," said Jared. "The pair of them settled this valley back in 1883."

"I thought your grandparents built the original

house." She'd seen the impressive structure when she first arrived this morning.

"The house, yes." He nodded downriver. "The original cabin's been abandoned for decades."

"So you're the fifth Ryder generation to live here?" Her article wasn't going to focus on the family history, but Melissa found herself fascinated by the thought of such deep roots.

"I'm the fifth," said Jared. "Tango's somewhere in the twenties."

"You've kept records?"

"Of course we've kept records." His tone told her she should have known that.

To cover the blunder, she turned and started walking down the rutted driveway, continuing her way toward the Windy River and the little white cottage she'd been assigned this morning. "How many horses do you have now?"

Jared fell into step beside her. "Several hundred. Several thousand head of cattle."

"Is the ranch still profitable?"

He hesitated, and she could feel him looking down at her. "Why do you ask?"

She kept her focus on the quarter moon riding above the silhouetted mountain range across the river. "You went into construction."

"How did you know that?"

"I heard people talk. Around the ranch."

"Gossip?"

"No," she quickly denied. "Just chitchat. You're here. You're usually in Chicago. People commented on it over lunch." Truth was, Melissa had carefully orchestrated the conversation that had revealed that information and more, but there was no need to mention that to Jared.

"You seem to know a lot about me."

She dared to look up at him. "You're the boss. People naturally care about what you do."

"They shouldn't."

She couldn't help but smile at that. "Maybe not. But that's not the way life works."

"It's gossip," he stated. "Plain and simple."

"It's curiosity," she corrected. "And it's interest. And respect."

He ground out an inarticulate sound.

"You can't make millions of dollars and hope to stay under the radar," she told him.

"How do you know I make millions of dollars?"

"How many acres you got here?"

"Five thousand."

"I rest my case."

"Most cattle ranches lose money these days."

"Most construction companies make money these days."

Jared didn't answer. They came up on the short bridge over the froth of a narrow spot in the river. A dirt driveway jutted off to the south, winding through a grass-and-wildflower carpet dotted with aspen and oak trees, which fronted the staff cabins. It looked exactly like the picture on the ranch Web site. This morning it had taken Melissa's breath away.

"Which is yours?" Jared asked, nodding to the neat row of white cottages.

"Number six."

"I'll walk you down." He turned on the driveway, and Melissa was struck by how easily he fit into the surroundings. He had a smooth, rolling, loose-limbed stride, and his booted feet never faltered on the uneven ground. A few lights burned behind curtained windows.

"Very gentlemanly of you." She hoped to keep him talking as long as possible.

"Wouldn't want you to run into a cougar." He seemed to be teasing, but it was hard to tell.

She decided to assume the ranch staff weren't in mortal danger this close to the buildings. "I'm more afraid of rogue cattle," she returned.

"The range bulls are up in the hills right now."

"Good to know. So how long are you in Montana?"

"About as long as you."

"Something you have to get back to?" She tripped on a tree root, and he quickly grasped her arm to steady her.

"Why do you ask?"

"Just making conversation. You seem to like it here."

He gazed around. The Windy River roared its way past, while an owl hooted in a faraway tree. A pair of truck lights flashed in the distance beyond the barns, while several horses whinnied to each other on the night air.

Melissa surreptitiously slowed her steps, not wanting to arrive at her cottage while Jared was still willing to talk.

"I've always liked it here." But his jaw was tight and his voice seemed strained.

Melissa sensed an undercurrent. "Why did you leave?" she dared.

"To make money," was the quick response.

"Cowboys need millions?"

"A spread this size needs millions. The past few decades have been hard on Montana ranchers. It'll change in the future. It has to. But for now…"

Her footsteps slowed to a stop. There was no help for it, they'd arrived at her front porch. She turned to face him, scrambling for ways to prolong the inevitable. She wasn't likely to get another chance like this for the rest of the week.

"So for now you're building office towers to keep your cattle ranch and horse-jumping operation in the black."

"How did you know I was building office towers?" The man was entirely too observant for her comfort level.

"Somebody also mentioned it at lunch today," she said, bluffing.

Jared stared into her eyes for a long slow moment. Then his index finger went to her chin and he tipped her face to the starlight. "There's something about you, Melissa."

"I'm a decent flirt?" Better to feed into his misconception than to let him start thinking about other possibilities.

He gazed at her a moment longer. "That must be it."

He paused again, his expression going unexpectedly intimate. "So you going to put out now?"

His voice was smooth, his dark eyes sensual, and his lips full and soft. Melissa let herself envision delivering with a kiss. Would it be soft and sweet? Strong and sure? Sensual? Sexy? Or downright erotic?

"You really are frighteningly good at this." His gruff voice interrupted her fantasy.

She blinked. "Huh?"

His jaw tightened, and he took a step back. "I can see why you've got so many men at your beck and call."

She shook her head. "I don't—"

"Be careful, Melissa," he warned. "Not all of them will walk away."

And with that, he turned on his heel.

She thought about calling out to protest. Her flirtation was normally light and inconsequential. She'd never let herself get carried away. This was the first time she'd ever even considered taking the next step.

And she wouldn't have actually kissed him.

There was far too much at stake. All she wanted was some information on his business, his life, his background.

And she had some.

Melissa couldn't help but smile.

Jared might think she was shameless, but at least he didn't know she was a journalist, and she'd obtained more useful material for her article.

Ignoring the anger in his stride, and the stiff set of his shoulders as he made his way back down the dirt driveway, she skipped up the stairs to her cottage. She needed to make notes right away.

"What did you do to tick Anthony off last night?" Stephanie's voice startled Jared as he tightened Tango's cinch in front of her house midmorning. The meeting had ended late last night, and it had been simpler to sleep here than ride ten miles to the main house at the cattle ranch in the dark. Anthony and Otto had left immediately after breakfast.

He took one final reflexive look at Melissa cleaning tack inside a shed across the driveway. The woman was taking an inordinately long time on a basic bridle. Then he slipped the cinch buckle into place and turned to face his sister.

Stephanie was dressed in dressage clothes, obviously ready for another day of training with Rosie-Jo. They had a competition coming up, but Jared couldn't remember the details.

"I told him to stop flirting with the help," Jared answered.

"What help?"

"Melissa." He pulled the right stirrup into place. "I don't know why you hired that woman. She's completely useless."

"She needed a job," said Stephanie.

"We're not running a charitable organization."

Stephanie stuffed one hand on her hip. "Actually we are."

Jared rolled his eyes, grasping the saddle horn to

wiggle it and test the placement. "Then she can apply through the Genevieve Fund."

"Don't be such a hard-ass."

"I'm not a hard-ass. I'm a realist." He nodded toward Melissa. "She's been working on that same bridle for half an hour. And mark my words, she's going to cause trouble between the cowboys."

"The cowboys are full-grown men."

"My point exactly."

"They're responsible for their own behavior."

Jared gave his sister a meaningful glare. Men were men. And flirtatious women were trouble. "Like I said, I'm a realist."

Stephanie set her helmet on the end post of the hitching rail and gathered her auburn hair into a ponytail. "I'm not going to fire Melissa."

"Well, I'm not going to be responsible for the fallout," he warned.

"Who said you had to be responsible? Besides, aren't you going back down to the cattle ranch today?"

Jared gently positioned the bit in Tango's mouth. "Thought I'd stay at your place for a few days."

There was a moment's silence, and he braced himself.

Her tone hardened. "I'm perfectly fine, big brother."

"I know you're perfectly fine," Jared allowed. He was sure she felt that way for now.

"This is no different than any other anniversary."

Jared didn't argue the point. But they'd just lost their grandfather, and Stephanie was hurting. No matter how hard she pretended otherwise, the siblings' annual reunion and visit to the family graveyard would be particularly difficult for her this year. He usually stayed down at the main house at the cattle ranch, since it was larger. But Stephanie couldn't leave her work and her students at the equestrian center, so he'd stay here instead.

"When's Royce showing up?" he asked, instead.

"Saturday. You should get back down there and help McQuestin." Stephanie referred to their aging cattle ranch manager.

"McQuestin doesn't want my help."

She plunked her helmet on her head and set her lips in a mulish line. "I don't need a babysitter."

Jared leaned back against the hitching rail, crossing his arms over his chest while he faced his sister. "Maybe I need you."

Her pale blue eyes immediately softened. "You *do?*"

He nodded. It wasn't a lie. He needed to be with her right now. It was the only way he'd be sure she was okay.

She moved forward and placed a hand on his arm. "I know you miss Gramps. Do you still miss Mom and Dad?"

Jared nodded again. But this time, his lie was outright. He didn't miss his parents. He was angry with his parents. Furious, if the truth be known. But that was his burden, the secret passed down by his grandfather. His only choice was to preserve their memories for his siblings.

Stephanie's eyes shimmered and she blinked rapidly. "Then you should stay."

Jared covered her hand with his. "Thank you."

"You want to watch me jump?"

"Sure." He nodded. "I'm going to check the pasture land at Buttercup Pond. Clear my head a little. I'll swing by later in the morning."

Stephanie nodded. Then she swiped the back of her hand across one cheek and headed for the main arena.

Jared tugged Tango's lead rope free and swung up into the saddle. The ride to Buttercup Pond to establish his cover story would take him a couple of hours. But his real mission was across the Windy River. Since his grandfather's deathbed revelation in April, he couldn't get his great-great-grandparents' cabin out of his mind.

The walk to the Ryders' great-great-grandparents' cabin took longer than Melissa had expected. At last she came around a bend of the river to see two cabins. One, made of logs, was nearly collapsing with age. The other was obviously newer. It was larger, made from lumber, with glass windows still intact and peeling white paint on the walls and porch.

A single story, it was L-shaped, with a peaked, green shingle roof. The rails had sagged off the porch, but the three steps looked safe enough, and the front door was a few inches ajar. The buildings were surrounded by a wildflower meadow that nestled up against steep rocky cliffs, jutting into the crystal-blue sky. The river glided by through a wide spot, nearly silent compared to the rapids upstream.

Melissa pulled out her cell phone, clicking a couple of pictures, wishing Susan was along with her camera.

Then she gingerly climbed the three stairs. She pressed the front door, slowly creaking it open. A dank, dusty room was revealed in the filtered sunlight through the stained windows. It held a stone fireplace, an aging dining table and chairs, and the remnants of a sofa. The floorboards were warped and creaky. Through a doorway, yellowed linoleum lined a small kitchen. Curtains hung in shreds over two of the windows.

Melissa let herself imagine the long-ago family. Jared's great-grandfather must have grown up here. Was he an only child? Did he have brothers and sisters? Did Jared have cousins and more-distant relatives around the country?

She made a mental note to research the family's genealogy.

On the far side of the living room, next to the kitchen door, a narrow hallway led to the other side of the house. The floor groaned under her running shoe–clad feet as she made her way through. Her movement stirred up dust, and she covered her mouth and nose with her hand to breathe more easily.

The hallway revealed two bedrooms. One was stark, with plywood bunks nailed to the wall and a hollow cutout of a closet. But the second was a surprise. Intact yellow curtains hung over the window. The bed was obviously newer than the other furnishings, and a brightly colored quilt was shoved against the brass footboard, while the remnants of two pillows were strewn at the head.

"Can I help you?"

The deep voice nearly scared Melissa out of her skin. Her hand flew to her heart as she whirled around to see Jared standing in the bedroom doorway.

"You scared me half to death!" she told him.

"Shouldn't you be working?"

"It's lunchtime. I thought you were a *ghost*." Her heart was still racing, and adrenaline prickled her skin, flushing her body, then cooling it rapidly.

"Still very much alive," he drawled, expression accusing. "What are you doing here?"

"I was curious."

He waited.

"Last night. You mentioned your great-great-grandparents and, well, I like old buildings."

"So you walked two miles?"

"Yes."

"On your lunch hour?"

"I wanted to come while it was light."

He sighed in disgust and gave his head a little shake. "You're flaky, you know that? Instead of eating, you take off on a whim to see a dilapidated old building. How are you going to work all afternoon?"

"I'll manage," she offered, already hungry and quite willing to concede his point. But she didn't have a lot of time to waste.

"You'll be passing out by two."

She could have argued, but she had more important

questions. "What's with this room?" She gestured around. "It seems newer."

Jared's gaze fixed on the disheveled bed for a long beat. His eyes hardened to sapphire, and a muscle ticked next to his left eye. "Must have been a staff member sleeping here."

"You think?" She wondered why they hadn't fixed up the rest of the house.

He seemed to guess her question. "I imagine they ate at the cookhouse with everybody else."

He turned his attention fully to Melissa and held out a broad callused hand. "Come on. I'll give you a lift home."

"You drove?" Why hadn't she heard the engine?

"I rode Tango."

She instinctively shrank back.

"Don't tell me you're afraid to ride double on him."

"Of course not." She sure hoped there wasn't a trick to riding double.

"Then let's go. You need to eat something."

"I'll be fi—"

"No, you won't. Skipping lunch was a stupid decision. Honestly, I don't know how you've managed to stay alive this long." He reached out and grasped her hand, tugging her out of the bedroom and down the hall.

"Did your great-grandfather have siblings?" she dared to ask.

"He had a sister."

"That explains the bunk beds."

"Yes, it does."

Melissa blinked in the strong sunlight, her focus going immediately to where Tango was tied to the porch.

Jared mounted, then maneuvered the horse flush against the railingless platform, holding out his hand.

Melissa took a deep breath. She braced herself against his forearm, then arced her right leg high, swinging her butt to land with an unladylike thud, off-center behind the saddle on Tango's broad back.

The horse grunted and stepped sideways.

Jared swore out loud, reached back to snag her waist and shoved her into place as her arms went instinctively around his body and clung tight.

"Sorry," she muttered against his back.

"You're a klutz," he told her. "On top of everything else, you're a klutz."

"I never learned to ride properly," she admitted.

"You need to learn some life skills," he responded. "I don't even care which ones. But damn, woman, you've got to learn how to do *something*."

He urged Tango into a fast walk. The motion and play of muscles were unsettling beneath Melissa's body. She kept her arms tight around Jared, slowly becoming aware of the intimacy of their position. Her breasts were plastered against his back, his cotton shirt and her T-shirt little barrier to the heat of their bodies. Her cheek rested against him, and every time she inhaled, her lungs were filled with his subtle, woodsy musk scent.

She was quickly getting turned on. Arousal boiled in the pit of her belly and tingled along her thighs. Her nipples had grown hard, and for a mortifying moment, she wondered if he could feel them.

"Where do you live in Indiana?" he asked, voice husky.

"Gary."

"You have a job there?"

"Not yet." She'd decided claiming to have a job would raise too many questions about why she needed money, and how she had enough time off to travel across the country.

"An apartment?"

"I've been staying with friends." Not having a job meant she couldn't claim to be paying rent. Unless she had investments or family money. In which case, she wouldn't need to earn money for a bus ticket.

As embarrassing as it might be, she had to pretend to be as big a loser as Jared had decided she was in order to maintain her cover story.

He grunted his disapproval, and she felt a twinge of regret that she couldn't set the record straight. But it wasn't her job to impress Jared Ryder. And it sure wasn't her job to be attracted to him. She'd have to fight her instincts on both fronts.

Four

Near the cookhouse, Jared helped Melissa down from Tango's back. She staggered to a standing position, and he could see the pain reflected in her expression as she stretched the muscles in her thighs. If the woman had ever been on a horse before, he'd eat saddle leather.

"*There* you are," came Stephanie's accusatory voice.

Jared felt a twinge of satisfaction at the thought of Melissa getting her comeuppance. But then he realized Stephanie was talking to him. He'd obviously missed her jumping practice.

"I gave Melissa a lift," he explained.

Stephanie looked at Melissa. "Are you hurt?"

"No, I was—"

"Downriver," Jared quickly put in. "Walking."

The explanation earned him a confused look from Melissa.

Too bad. He'd worry about that one later. For now, he didn't want to plant any thoughts about the old cabin in Stephanie's head.

Stephanie looked from Jared to Melissa, then back again. "Well, you missed a no-fault round," she told him, putting her pert nose in the air.

"I guess you'll just have to do it again."

"You think it's easy?"

"No," he acknowledged. "I think it's very, very hard. But I also know you're a perfectionist."

"I wish," Stephanie retorted. But Jared knew it was true. You didn't become one of the top-ten show jumpers in the country without a strong streak of perfectionism.

He handed Tango's reins to Melissa. "He's all yours. When you're done taking off the tack, put him back in the red-gated pen."

Melissa glanced down at the leather reins. Then she looked at Jared, her eyes widening with trepidation.

Yeah, he thought so.

He gave a heavy sigh and took back the reins. "Or I could give you a hand," he offered. "Then you can grab something to eat."

He felt Stephanie's curious gaze behind him, and he twisted his head to give her an I-told-you-so stare. If she wanted him to have time to watch her jump, she shouldn't have hired such a hopeless case.

He wrapped the reins around the horn of his saddle,

clipped a lead rope onto Tango's bridle, then walked the few steps to the hitching rail in front of the stable.

"You can start with the cinch," he called over his shoulder, and Melissa quickly scrambled into action, hoofing it across the loose-packed dirt of the pen.

Stephanie watched them for a moment longer. Then he saw a small, hopeful smile quirk the corners of her mouth before she turned away.

Great. His good deed was obviously not going to go unpunished. He was helping Melissa out of pity, not out of attraction. She might be a gorgeous woman, but he liked his dates with a little more gray matter and a whole lot more ambition.

She came to a halt a few feet back from Tango's flank. Her hands curled into balls by her sides, strands of her blond hair fluttering across her flushed cheeks as she blinked at the tall black horse.

"The cinch," Jared prompted, releasing the reins and gently drawing the bit from Tango's mouth.

Melissa didn't make a move.

He flipped the stirrup up and hooked it over the saddle horn. "The big, shiny silver buckle," he offered sarcastically.

She took a half step forward, then wiped her palms down the front of her jeans.

Jared turned, planting his hands on his hips.

She pursed her lips, reaching her hand toward the buckle. But Tango shifted, and she snapped it back.

"He's not going to bite you."

"What if he kicks me?"

"Just don't do anything sudden."

"Oh, that makes me feel a whole lot better."

This was getting ridiculous. "You know, you might want to think about another line of work."

"I was perfectly happy scooping out pens."

"Nobody's happy scooping out pens."

"I was."

"Well, that's a dead-end career." He took a step forward and captured her hand.

She tried to jerk away.

"The trick is," said Jared in the most soothing voice he could muster, "to let him know what you're doing." He urged her reluctant hand toward Tango's withers. "That way, nobody is surprised."

"Is 'surprised' a euphemism?"

"I mean it literally."

Tango craned his neck to see what was going on.

"Your touch should be firm," Jared advised, keeping himself between Melissa and the horse's head. He gave Tango a warm-up pat with his free hand before placing Melissa's palm on the horse's coat. "That way, he knows you have confidence."

"I don't have confidence."

"Sure you do." He let go of her hand, and she immediately pulled it back from the horse.

Jared drew a frustrated sigh. "I've seen five-year-olds with more guts than you."

She glared at him.

"Lots of them," he affirmed.

Her glare lasted several seconds longer, but then she squared her shoulders, screwed up her face and turned to the saddle.

"Buckle first," Jared instructed as her small soft fingers tackled the leather. "Now pull the strap through the rings."

It took her a minute to get the mohair strap untangled and dangling straight down.

"You want to take the saddle and blanket off together. Grab it front and back. Lift, don't drag it. Then carry it into the stable. I'll show you where to put it."

He stepped back to give her some room.

Tango was sixteen hands, so it was a reach for Melissa to get a firm grip. But she grabbed the saddle, lifted, pulled back, stumbled in the loosely packed dirt and nearly fell over backward.

Jared quickly wrapped his arm around the small of her back, averting disaster. Her waist was small, her body and frame light. No wonder she was such a wimp when it came to physical work.

"You okay?" he asked reflexively.

"Fine." She firmed up her grip on the heavy saddle and straightened away before he could get used to the feel of her in his arms. But not before he realized how easily he could get used to the feel of her in his arms.

He wondered if she danced. Then for a second he allowed himself to imagine her in a dress. A dress would suit her, something silky and flowing, maybe a bright blue or magenta. Despite her hesitancy in the stable yard, something told him she'd have self-confidence in a different setting.

She all but staggered into the stable, and he was forced to give her points for grit.

"Third rack from the end," he instructed, following with the reins.

She plunked the saddle down.

"You can clean it after lunch," he told her.

She nodded, obviously out of breath. Then she dusted off the front of her navy tank top.

"But first we move Tango."

"Of course we do." Her tone was sarcastic as she turned to face him.

"You ticked off at me? For helping you?"

She studied his eyes. "No." But the tone told him she was.

"You can always quit."

"I'm not going to quit." Her annoyance was replaced by defiance as she started for the stable door. "Let's go."

"You want to lead him from the left," Jared called after her as he hung up the reins, positive now that she'd never been near a horse before today.

Tango wasn't intimidating. He was an incredibly well-trained, twelve-year-old saddlebred, solid as a rock and not the least bit flighty or malicious. Any horseman, groom or stable hand would recognize that in an instant.

He came through the doorway to find Melissa sizing up Tango from about five feet away.

"Talk to him," Jared advised. "Then give him a pat and undo the rope."

"Is there a trick to it?" she asked, apparently having given up any pretext of knowing what she was doing.

"Which part?"

Over her shoulder, she cut him an impatient glare, and he was forced to tamp down a smile.

"Pull the end." He demonstrated, tugging the quick-release knot. Then he handed her the rope. "Stand on this side. Make sure he can see you. Don't let the rope trail." Jared got her positioned properly. He didn't know how much she'd have to work between here and Seattle, but she stood a much better chance of avoiding starvation if she had a clue about what she was doing.

Melissa started walking, and Tango fell in easily beside her. Her face was pinched and pale, and there was clear tension across her slim shoulders as she made her way toward the ranch road, but at least she was making the effort.

A couple of Stephanie's border collies streaked toward them, obviously assuming there was work to be done. Melissa tensed, and Jared put an arm around her. "They won't hurt you."

"I know."

"You do?"

"They look…friendly." But her voice was slightly higher pitched than normal. "Will they scare Tango?"

"Tango's bomb-proof."

The dogs circled the small group a couple of times, then settled in back of Tango's heels, obviously up for whatever the job might be.

Melissa led the horse in silence down the slight slope of the dirt road, curving east toward the river and a row of horse pens. Stephanie was teaching a junior jumping class in the main arena behind them. The Ryder farrier was working on a yearling with the help of two cowboys who were trying to teach the twitchy colt the proper etiquette for hoof care. Meanwhile, stable hands moved hay, filled water troughs and repaired fences.

There was an endless cycle of work on a horse ranch. When he was in the city, Jared missed the predictable rhythm. In his corporate life, he was putting out one fire after another. He couldn't plan a single day, never mind a season.

"Did you come to an agreement about Tappee?" she asked as they approached the red-gated pen.

Jared shook his head, increasing his pace to unlatch the gate in front of the horse. "Stephanie voted with me, but Otto sided with Anthony."

"Otto?"

"Otto Durand."

Her forehead furrowed as she cautiously led Tango through the gate. "I don't understand."

Jared pulled it shut and flipped the latch. "There's a clip under his chin. Release the lead rope."

She reached cautiously under the horse's head. But she found the clip and clicked it free.

Tango instantly reacted to the familiar sound. Knowing he was free, he bolted, spraying clods of dirt at Melissa.

It was all Jared could do not to laugh at the horrified expression on her face.

She sputtered out the dirt while the horse rolled onto his back, relieved to be free of the saddle.

"What don't you understand?" he asked, instead.

She brushed away her hair and rubbed the back of

her hand over her face. "I don't understand why you had to vote. Aren't you CEO of Ryder International?"

"This isn't a Ryder International project."

"Oh. I thought…"

Jared cracked the gate open to man-size so they could exit the pen. "It's the Genevieve Fund."

Melissa raised her brow in a question.

"The Genevieve Ryder Memorial Fund," Jared explained. "It's a charitable trust named after my mother."

"Is your mother…?"

He nodded. "She was killed twenty years ago."

Her forehead creased. "I'm sorry."

Jared shrugged, brushing past the sharp stab of conflicting emotions that tightened his chest. "It's been twenty years."

Melissa's green eyes were round and soft. Her voice dropped to a husky level that somehow hit him in the solar plexus. "I'm still sorry."

They stared at each other in silence, and once again he was struck by the intelligence in her eyes. Only this time, it was laced with compassion. There was something he didn't understand about this woman, something lurking just beyond his comprehension.

"There are five members of the Genevieve Fund board," he told her, leaning an arm on a fence rail, forcing the frustrating dilemma from his head.

"Who's the fifth?" She mirrored his posture.

"My brother, Royce."

"I take it he gets to break the tie?"

"He'll be here on Saturday."

"Does he work on the ranch or with the construction company?"

"Neither. He works for Ryder International, but he's involved in acquisitions, not in the day-to-day business."

"So he was the one who found Saxena Electronics?"

And there it was again. "How do you know about Saxena?"

"I told you, Jared." She smoothed her mussed hair back from her forehead. "I read the newspapers."

"And you remember obscure facts like that?"

She shrugged. "Sometimes it's a blessing. Sometimes it's a curse."

"Ever heard of Bosoniga?"

"Little country in West Africa." She grinned, revealing flashing white teeth. "Is this a quiz?"

"We're building a school there."

Her head bobbed up and down. "Good choice. The monarchy is stable, so poverty and infrastructure will be your only problems."

He lifted his hand, then brought it down again on the rough wood of the fence, struggling to make Melissa's lifestyle add up in his head. "Why don't you have a real job?"

"Define a real job."

"An office, where'd you put that brain of yours to work from nine to five."

"I don't think they'd let me wander across the country."

"How long have you been wandering across the country?"

Her mouth tightened imperceptibly, and something flashed in the depths of her eyes. Fear? Pain? He was reminded once again that she could be running from something or someone.

But then the look was gone.

"Not long," she answered. "Do you think Royce will side with his family or with Anthony and Otto?"

"Anthony is our cousin."

"Really?"

He nodded. "Royce is a risk taker. He'll offer to fly down to Tappee himself."

"He's a pilot?"

Jared choked out a laugh. "He's definitely a pilot. I think he likes flying around the world more than he likes investigating companies."

"Can I meet him when he gets here?"

Jared tensed. A chill hit his body, and a warning sparked in his brain. "Why?"

She drew back, obviously reacting to his expression.

"You planning to flirt with him?" Jarred pressed. He shouldn't have let his guard down. He didn't know anything about this woman.

She emphatically shook her head. "He likes to travel. I like to travel." Her words came faster. "I was thinking you could be right. Maybe I should find a real job and save up some money. I mean, seeing America is fun and all, but it might be fun to see some of the rest of the world—"

"In my brother's jet?"

"No. *No*." She smoothed her hair back again. "I'm not going to flirt with your brother. I just thought…"

Jared waited. He truly did want to know what she thought.

She let go of the fence rail and took a step forward. "I thought he might be a lot like you. Smart and interesting."

He stared down as she moved closer. "I can't believe you're doing this." But what he really couldn't believe was that it was working. She was flirting with him, using her pretty face and killer body to gain an advantage. And it was *working*.

He was pathetic.

"You misunderstood," she told him in a soft voice. "I have no designs on Royce. I don't even know Royce. And if my mission was to land myself a rich man, do you think I'd be scooping horse poop on a ranch in Montana? No offense, Jared, but Manhattan is a whole lot closer to Gary, and their per capita count of rich eligible men is pretty darn high."

Jared watched her soft lips as they formed words, took in her feathery hair lifting in the light breeze, her bottomless green eyes, almost a turquoise, like the newly melted water of a glacial lake. She was stunningly gorgeous and intriguingly intelligent.

"So how stupid do you think I am?" Her voice dropped off into silence. The thuds of Tango's footfalls echoed around them.

"I don't think you're stupid at all," Jared admitted. "That's the problem."

* * *

Melissa had overplayed her hand.

Sitting at the end of a long table in the quiet cookhouse, spooning her way through a flavorful soup, she knew she'd made Jared suspicious. She should never have asked to meet Royce. And she should have been content to let him think she was slow-witted.

Her enthusiasm for getting the story, along with her stupid ego, had both gotten in the way. She'd just *had* to show off her knowledge of Bosoniga and Tappee. Like some schoolkid trying to impress the teacher. "Bosoniga has a stable monarchy," she mocked under her breath. Why didn't she just wave her university degree under his nose and challenge him to guess why she was out on the road playing vagabond?

She dropped the spoon into her soup.

Was she trying to sabotage the story?

"Melissa?" Someone slid into the chair next to her, and Melissa looked over to see Stephanie set a white stonewear cup on the table.

At two in the afternoon, the cookhouse had grown quiet. Faint voices could be heard from the pass-through to the kitchen. Coffee, biscuits and oatmeal cookies were still available on the sideboard in case anyone needed a snack. And a helper was setting the three empty tables for dinner.

"Hello," Melissa greeted Stephanie politely.

The younger woman's auburn hair was pulled back in her signature ponytail. She'd removed her riding helmet, but still wore the white blouse, tight jodhpurs and high boots that were the uniform of a show jumper.

Stephanie grinned happily. There was a freshness about her, Melissa thought. Maybe it was the freckles or maybe it was the complete lack of cosmetics. Or it could have been the perky upturned nose. But Stephanie looked young, carefree, almost mischievous.

"I saw Jared helping you with Tango," she began, her expression friendly and open as she turned the cup handle to face the right direction.

Melissa nodded, even while her stomach tightened with guilt. She couldn't help but like Stephanie, and she was sorry the woman was caught up in her charade.

"It was very nice of him," Melissa acknowledged. Then she paused, choosing her words carefully. "My horse skills are..." She let out a sigh, feeling like a heel for lying to Stephanie in the first place. "I guess, I, uh, exaggerated my skill level when I first talked to you." She cringed, waiting for the reaction.

But to her surprise, Stephanie waved a dismissive hand. "Whatever."

Melissa gazed at her. "But—"

"It doesn't take a rocket scientist to shovel manure."

"You're not mad?"

"Nah." Stephanie lifted the stonewear mug and took a sip of the steaming coffee. "I imagine people exaggerate on their résumés all the time."

"I guess they do," Melissa agreed, relieved—yet again—that she wasn't about to get fired.

"So what do you think of him?"

"Tango?" Was Stephanie going to try to get her to ride the horse?

"No, Jared."

"Oh." Melissa caught the speculative expression in Stephanie's eyes.

Oh.

Oh, no.

This could not be good.

"He seems, well, nice enough," Melissa offered carefully. Truth was, she thought Jared was demanding and sarcastic. Okay, in an intriguing, compelling, sexy kind of way.

Stephanie nodded cheerily. "He's a great guy. Lots of women seem attracted to him. I mean, it's hard for me to tell, being his sister, but I imagine he's pretty hot."

Melissa turned her attention back to her soup. "He's a very attractive man."

"You should have seen the woman he dated last weekend. They had their picture in the paper in Chicago. She was a knockout. A lawyer."

Melissa spooned up a bit of soup. She was not going to be jealous of some smart knockout lawyer in Chicago. Who Jared dated was absolutely none of her business.

"I told him he should see her again. But he's not interested." Stephanie gave a shrug. "So, really, he's not committed in any way, shape or form."

Melissa fought a smile. Again, there was an endearing quality to Stephanie. She was probably only four or five years younger than Melissa, but she seemed so innocent and untarnished. Maybe it was from living in the protected world of rural Montana.

"Honestly, Stephanie, I think I frustrate your brother."

Stephanie shook her head. "We can change that."

"I'm only here for a few days, remember?" The last thing Melissa needed was for Stephanie to give Jared a reason to avoid her. And she sensed that was exactly what would happen if he guessed his sister's intentions.

"He thinks you're pretty."

The assertion took Melissa by surprise.

"He told me," Stephanie continued. "The first time he saw you."

"This is a bad idea, Stephanie. Jared and I are from completely different worlds." And she was spying on him. And he was going to despise her in about three weeks when the article hit the newsstands.

"So were my parents."

"Stephanie, really."

"My dad was a rancher, and my mom grew up in Boston."

Melissa knew this was exactly the point where she should press Stephanie for some information. But for some reason, she couldn't bring herself to do it.

"My mom was gorgeous and classy. Blonde, like you." Stephanie sighed. "I wish I looked more like her."

"But you're beautiful," Melissa immediately put in, meaning it completely.

Stephanie wrinkled her little nose. "I have freckles and red hair. And, you know, I haven't bought myself a dress in three years."

"Well, that's easy to fix."

"I bet you own a lot of beautiful dresses." The speculative look was back in Stephanie's eyes.

"Very few," said Melissa. She pinned Stephanie with an earnest expression. "Promise me you won't do this, Stephanie."

Stephanie reached out to grasp Melissa's forearm, taking a careful look around the room. "I can be very discreet."

Given the woman's exaggerated spy-versus-spy room check, Melissa sincerely doubted that.

"I'll chat you up a bit," Stephanie continued. "You are gorgeous, and I can—"

"Jared is not, I repeat, not interested in me. You'll only embarrass us both if you try to match us up."

Stephanie took another sip of her coffee, a dreamy faraway expression in her eyes. "I promise, Melissa. I won't do a single thing to embarrass you."

Five

Melissa had waited all morning for a chance to privately warn Jared about Stephanie's matchmaking plans. She could hardly walk up to the front door of Stephanie's house and knock. And Jared, as far as she could tell, hadn't come out of the house.

Standing over a tub of water in the tack room, she had a decent view of the front porch. Her hands were red and slippery from the glycerin soap, but at least the job was straightforward: wash the tack, dry the tack, polish the tack. She'd worked her way through a decent-size pile of leather.

When lunchtime came along without a sign of Jared, she started to worry. If Stephanie was already matchmaking, he was probably plotting his escape from the equestrian center. If she didn't do something soon, there was every possibility that he'd leave before she got anything more for her story.

She had to find a way to get hold of him.

She clicked through the possibilities in her brain until finally she came up with a viable plan. If she could somehow get her hands on his cell number, she could talk to him without Stephanie knowing.

She pulled her hands from the warm water, shook them off and dried them on a towel. Her cell phone was in her taupe canvas tote bag, and it didn't take her long to get directory assistance and the Chicago number for Ryder International. The receptionist put her through to Jared's assistant.

"Jared Ryder's office," said a friendly female voice.

"I need to speak to Jared Ryder," Melissa opened, hoping the office would give her his cell phone number.

"I'm afraid Mr. Ryder is not in the office today." The voice remained friendly and professional. "Can I help you with something?"

"Do you happen to have his cell phone number?" Melissa mentally crossed her fingers that the woman would be willing to give it out.

"I'm afraid I can't provide that information. Is there someone else who can—"

"Would you be able to get a message to him?" Melissa moved to plan B.

Some of the patience leached out of the woman's voice. "Can I get your name, please?"

"So you can get him a message?" Melissa's hope rose.

"He may not get it until next week."

"I need him to get it today. Right away if possible."

"If I could just have your name."

"It's Melissa. Melissa Webster." She used the alias she'd used on her résumé.

"And what is the message regarding?"

Good question. Melissa racked her brain. She sure couldn't say she was a reporter, but if the subject didn't seem important, the secretary might not send it to Jared right away. "Saxena Electronics," she offered impulsively.

"You're from Saxena?" The skepticism was clear.

Melissa could only assume most Saxena employees had East Indian accents. "I'm affiliated with them," she lied. "The message is that Melissa Webster needs to talk about Saxena right away. In private," she added, ending with her cell phone number.

"I'm not sure—"

"Please believe me that it's important," Melissa put in quickly.

The woman hesitated on the other end of the line.

"There's no risk," Melissa pointed out. "If it's not important, he'll just ignore it, right?"

"I'll see what I can do."

"Maybe a quick text or an e-mail?"

"I'll see what I can do." The voice had turned stony.

It was definitely time to back off. "Thank you," said Melissa with as much gratitude as she could muster. "I really do appreciate this."

The professionalism and the formality came back. "Thank you for calling Ryder International."

"Thanks for your help," Melissa offered once more before hanging up.

Then she plunked her phone back in her bag, readjusted the clip that was holding her hair back and pulled her damp tank top away from her chest. She hated to go to lunch looking like this, but it was a long walk back to her cottage, and there was no way she could skip the meal.

As the days went by, her respect for cowboys and stable hands had risen. They worked extremely hard. A salad or a protein shake might cut it in an office, but out here, calories were essential.

She dried the last of the washed tack, laying it out on the bench to be polished later. Then she slung her canvas bag over her shoulder and headed for the cookhouse while she waited to see if Jared would call.

A couple of steps out the stable door, Jared startled her, blocking her way. She stopped short.

"What the hell?" he demanded.

She glanced around. "Is Stephanie with you?"

"What was this about seeing me in private?"

She didn't see Stephanie anywhere. "I'll explain in a minute. Is there somewhere we can talk?"

Jared hesitated. Then he nodded at the stable. "There's an office up those stairs."

"Great." Melissa turned, and he followed her in.

They tapped their way, single file, up the narrow staircase. It opened to a short hallway with three doors.

"Far end," Jared rumbled. "And this better be good. My secretary was scrambling the Saxena team for damage control. She thought you were warning me of a hostile takeover."

Melissa cringed. "Sorry. Did you call them off?"

"Of course I called them off." His boots were heavy on the wood floor behind her. "This better not be some flirting thing."

"It's not flirting." Melissa stopped at the closed door.

Jared reached around her and pushed it open to reveal a small desk, a couple of filing cabinets. Three open, curtained windows showed a cloud-laden sky, and a comfortably furnished corner with armchairs, low tables and lamps. Through the window, Melissa could see a crowd of people at the arena. She assumed it was a jumping class and that Stephanie was there.

"Take a seat." Jared gestured to a worn, brown leather armchair.

Melissa sat down, and he took the chair next to it. They were separated by a polished pine table, decorated with three small, framed horse portraits.

He leaned back, crossing one ankle over the opposite knee and folding his arms over his chest. "What's going on?" he asked directly.

Melissa took a deep breath, giving herself a second to compose her message. "It's Stephanie."

"What did you do?"

"I didn't do anything."

"She lost patience with you? Fired you?"

"No." Melissa sat forward. "Will you let me finish?"

He waited.

"Your sister, for some reason, has decided I'm...well, a good match for you."

Jared planted his feet and sat forward. "What did you say to her?"

"Nothing. This is about her, not me. I was minding my own business. She saw you helping me yesterday. Apparently the first time you saw me you said I was pretty."

"I never—"

"Well, Stephanie thinks you did. And she's a determined and romantic young lady, and she thinks she can subtly throw us together without you noticing. I was guessing you'd catch on, and I thought you'd appreciate a heads-up."

Jared's mouth thinned into a grim line. His hands moved to the arms of the chair, and he gave his head a subtle shake. "It's worse than I thought."

Melissa waited for him to elaborate.

He fixed his gaze on her. "If she's targeting *you,* things are really getting out of hand."

"Excuse me?" Melissa couldn't help the defensive tone in her voice. "I'm the bottom of the barrel?"

"No, you're not the bottom of the barrel." He paused. "But you're definitely from the unlikely half of the barrel."

"Is that supposed to make me feel better?"

"The last person she targeted was a lawyer."

Melissa nodded. "She told me."

"Just how long was this conversation?"

"Not long." Melissa shifted back in her chair. "For the record, I tried to talk her out of it."

Jared's expression turned thoughtful, and he glanced toward the window and out to the arena. "Did she seem...upset?"

Melissa shook her head. Stephanie hadn't seemed remotely upset. "I'd call it enthusiastic, even excited."

He stood up and walked toward the closest window, looking through the opening to the crowd in the distance. "It's about Sunday."

Melissa stood with him. The clouds were thickening in the sky and the wind was picking up.

"It's got to be," he continued.

"What about Sunday?" she dared to ask.

Jared kept his gaze glued outside. "The twentieth anniversary of our parents' deaths. And the first time my grandfather won't be here to commemorate it with us."

Melissa took a few steps toward him. "Your grandfather died?"

Jared nodded. "In April. It hit Stephanie pretty hard."

"I can imagine," Melissa said softly, her sympathy going out to the whole family.

"Look at her jump." Jared nodded toward the arena, and Melissa shifted closer to where she could watch Stephanie on her big gray horse.

"Perfect form," he continued as the two sailed over a high, white jump rail. "She's talented, driven, unbelievably hardworking. Only twenty-two, and she'll be a champion before we know it."

"Then she was only two when your parents died?" Melissa ventured.

"Only two," Jared confirmed with a nod, and his voice turned introspective. "And despite her success, all these years all she ever wanted was a mother."

Melissa didn't know what to say to that. Her own parents had moved to Florida only a couple of years ago. She saw them every few months, but she still missed her mother.

"I don't blame her," she offered.

"I understand the desire," Jared allowed. "But ever since she was old enough to understand, she's pestered the three of us to get married. Poor Gramps. And poor Royce. He was afraid to bring a date home in high school for fear of how Stephanie would embarrass him. She goes into matchmaking mode at the drop of a hat."

"You could get married, you know," Melissa offered reasonably, only half joking. "You're what, early thirties?"

"Thirty-five."

"So what's the holdup? I bet you meet eligible women every day of the week."

Jared frowned at her. "I'm not getting married for the sake of my sister."

"Get married for yourself. Hey, if you get proactive, you'll have your choice of women. If Stephanie gets her way, you're stuck with me."

It obviously took Jared a stunned minute to realize Melissa was joking. But then he visibly relaxed.

"What about you?" he asked. "Would you get married to keep your siblings happy?"

Melissa coughed out a laugh. "I have five older brothers. Trust me, no husband in the world will be good enough."

"Would they scare a guy off?"

Melissa smiled at that. "They range from six-one to six-four. All tough as nails. Adam's a roofer, Ben and Caleb are framers, Dan's an electrician and Eddy's a pipe fitter."

A calculating look came into Jared's eyes. "You think they'd be interested in jobs with Ryder International?"

"I'm afraid they're all gainfully employed."

His eyes squinted down as he stared at her, and she braced herself for sarcasm about her own dismal career status. It was going to be hard not to defend herself from his criticism.

"Might be worth marrying you for the union connections alone."

The words surprised a laugh out of her. She played along. "Plus, Stephanie would have a mother." She played along. "Well, more like a sister, really. I'm only four or five years older than she is, you know."

"Not a bad plan." Jared nodded and pretended to give it serious consideration. "Stephanie's pretty convinced the family would benefit from a few more females in the mix."

"Smart girl," said Melissa.

"Can't argue with the logic," Jared agreed. "It's her methods that cause the trouble."

As they spoke, Stephanie sailed over her final jump, completing a clean round.

"She really is good," said Melissa.

"You don't know the half of it." Jared turned from the window.

He paused, and they came face-to-face, closer than she'd realized. Sunlight streamed in, highlighting his gorgeous eyes, his strong chin, his straight nose and the short shock of brown hair that curled across his forehead.

The force of his raw magnetism drew her in, arousing and frightening her at the same time. He was all man. He had power, looks and intelligence, and she suddenly felt inadequate. She wasn't ready to work at his ranch or write an article about him. The phrase *out of my league* planted itself firmly in her brain.

For a second she let herself fear his reaction to the article. But then she banished the fear. It was her job to get the story, and she'd be far away from Montana by the time it ran in the *Bizz*.

The world outside darkened, and his eyes turned to midnight, sensuality radiating from their depths. The humidity jumped up, only to be overtaken by a freshening breeze.

There were shouts from outside as the wind swirled and a storm threatened. Doors banged, horses whinnied, and plastic tarps rattled against their ropes.

Meanwhile, gazes locked, Jared and Melissa didn't move.

The wild clamor outside matched the cacophony inside her head. This attraction felt so right, but it was so incredibly wrong. Jared was her article subject, her employer, one of the most powerful entrepreneurs in Chicago. She had absolutely no business being attracted to him.

He reached out to brush a stray lock of hair from her temple. His touch was electric, arousing, light as a feather but shocking as a lightning bolt.

Thunder rumbled in the distance, and the first fat raindrops clattered on the roof.

"I'm going to kiss you," he told her.

She drew a breath. "You think that's a good idea?"

He moved slightly closer. "It's not the smartest thing I've ever done." He stroked his thumb along her jaw, tipped her chin. "But probably not the stupidest, either. Might not even make the top three."

"What were they?" she asked.

"The stupidest things?"

She gave a slight nod.

"I don't think I'll be telling you that right now."

"Maybe later?"

"I doubt it." Done talking, he leaned in and pressed his warm lips to hers.

It was a gentle kiss, a tentative kiss. There was a wealth of respect and more than a couple of questions contained in the kiss.

She answered by softening her lips. One of her hands went to his shoulder, steadying herself, she lied. Truth was, she wanted to hang on, press closer, turn his inquiry into a genuine kiss.

He easily complied, stepping forward, parting his lips, one hand going to the small of her back, the other tunneling into the hair behind her ear. He tipped his head, deepened the kiss; she plastered herself flush against him, feeling the hard heat of his body, counterpoint to the wind and rain that rushed in through the open window.

Warning sirens clanged inside her head.

It wasn't supposed to happen like this.

She was supposed to maintain a journalistic detachment. Plus, hadn't she come up here to warn him about Stephanie? Not to flirt. Or worse, seduce. What on earth was she *thinking?*

He broke the kiss, but moved instantly into another. Melissa didn't have time to decide if she was relieved or upset before she was dragged away on another tidal wave of desire.

The world disappeared—the horses, the people, the wind and rain. Nothing existed except Jared's kiss, the rough texture of his hands, the heat of his hard body and the fresh, earthy, male scent that surrounded her and drew her into an alternative universe.

His thumb found the strip of skin between her tank top and blue jeans. He stroked up her spine, sending shivers of reaction skittering both ways. His hand slipped under her shirt, warm palm caressing the sensitized skin, working higher, closing in on the scrap of her bra.

His tongue touched hers, tentatively at first, but then bolder as she responded, opening to him, tipping her head to give him better access to her mouth. His hand caressed the back of her head. Her arms tightened around his neck. She went up on her toes, struggling to get closer.

A clap of thunder boomed through the sky, rumbling the building, lightning dancing in the clouds rapidly engulfed the ranch. The rain grew steady, blurring the world, cooling the air and clattering like a freight train against the cedar shakes above them.

Jared pulled her tighter still, leaving her in no doubt about the effect the kiss was having on him. It was having the same effect on her. It was wild, untamed, sexy and all but unstoppable.

He shifted, moving her away from the open window and the driving rain that was dampening their clothes. He backed her into the wall, and his leg slipped between hers. The friction sent a shot of desire through her body, and a moan found its way past her mouth.

Jared whispered her name, his kisses moving from her mouth to her cheek, her temple and neck. He moved aside the strap of her tank top, the thinner strap of her bra, kissing his way to her shoulder, where his warm tongue lingered, laving the sensitive skin.

Her legs grew weak, and she braced herself against the wall, clinging to Jared's strong shoulders, even as she kissed his chest through the damp cotton of his shirt. He'd crooked his knee, and she rested the core of her body against his strong thigh. A pulse throbbed through her veins, and there was no mistaking where she wanted this to lead.

"We have to stop," she forced herself to gasp.

His lips paused mid-kiss on her bare shoulder. "I'm not sure why," he breathed. He straightened, bracing his hands against the wall, arms on either side of her, gazing down with passion-clouded eyes.

"Did I do something wrong?" he asked.

She was all but shaking with reaction, afraid to move for fear she'd throw caution to the wind and lose herself in his arms. "This is nuts," she told him, struggling to bring her voice back to normal, forcing herself to drag her hands from his shoulders.

His thigh was still braced between hers, still pressed intimately against her body, still drawing a completely inappropriate reaction from her.

"Why?" he asked.

"I don't know," she nearly wailed. What had happened? Why had they combusted like that? They barely knew each other.

"I mean, why is it nuts?"

"Because..." She struggled over the question, not finding a satisfactory answer. At least, not one that she could share with him. "It's you, and it's me. And we're..." She couldn't find the words.

"Attracted to each other?" he finished for her.

"Apparently," she responded dryly.

He let his thigh fall away, and she nearly groaned with the sensation.

"Stephanie would be pleased," he pointed out.

Melissa's gaze darted to the window, suddenly wondering who had seen what before they moved away. What if Stephanie had seen them?

"Nobody saw a thing," said Jared, guessing her concern. "They were too busy running from the storm."

The rain had turned to a steady drum, while thunder and lightning punctuated the darkened sky. The yard was empty, everyone having taken shelter in one of the buildings. Horses were huddled in small groups, most of them under run-in shelters, some in the larger pens moving into the shelter of the trees. Tarps still billowed, cracking and snapping in the wind.

Jared gently stroked his thumb across her swollen bottom lip, making her desire flare all over again. "Our secret is safe."

She gazed into his eyes, unable to hide her renewed longing. And try as she might, she couldn't bring herself to walk away.

His eyes darkened further and his voice went husky. "You want to make it an even bigger secret?"

Six

Before Melissa could even open her mouth, Jared knew to retract the question.

"I'm sorry," he quickly told her. "That was way out of line."

He was her boss. Just yesterday he'd threatened to fire her, more than once, if memory served. He had absolutely no business propositioning her. It was unprincipled, immoral, probably illegal in most states.

"It wasn't—"

"It *was.*" He forced himself back, hands tightening by his sides as he put some distance between them. The torrential rain was still dripping through the open windows, and he slammed one window shut, then the next and finally the third, taking some of his frustration out on the inanimate objects. He'd never felt this way before, never desired a woman so quickly and thoroughly. Yet he was wrong to feel this way, and he had to make it stop.

"Jared?" Her voice was tentative, and he felt like a complete jerk.

He latched the final window, then turned back to face her. Her hair was wet, messy from his hands. The damp blue tank top clung to her breasts, highlighting her nipples. Her eyes were round, sea-foam green and confused.

"I'm mad at myself," he assured her. "Not at you."

She took a step forward. "It was my fault, too. How about we forget it happened?"

"Can *you* forget it happened?" He'd give it a shot, but he wasn't holding out much hope.

"Sure." She nodded, offering a small smile. "Easy."

She seemed sincere, and he tried not to be offended. Maybe he'd imagined their explosive passion. Maybe to her it had been a simple ordinary kiss. He gave himself a split second to ponder exactly who the hell else she'd been kissing like that, but then he acknowledged that it was none of his business.

He took a deep breath, forcing himself to relax. "Sure," he forced out, adjusting his damp shirt and raking his fingers through his hair. "We'll just forget it ever happened."

Melissa glanced down and plucked at her own wet shirt. Then she quickly folded her arms across her breasts. Just as well, Jared told himself. Her clinging clothes were turning him on. So were her swollen lips and messy hair.

"You have a comb?" he asked.

She shook her head. "It's in my bag downstairs."

He realized they couldn't risk leaving the room with her looking like this, so he steeled himself against the inevitable reaction and moved toward her.

Her arms stayed protectively crossed over her breasts, so he reached for the hair clip. "I'll just…" He raked spread fingers through the mess, straightening out the worst of it, wondering how he'd ever manage to get the clip back in.

A voice called from the hallway. *"Jared?"* The door burst open, and Stephanie instantly appeared.

He and Melissa both jumped guiltily back, her covering her breasts, him holding her hair clip.

Stephanie stopped abruptly. "I'm sorry." But she didn't look sorry in the least. A broad grin grew on her face and her eyes sparkled in delight.

Barry Salmon and Hal Norris halted behind her. All three of them stared at the incriminating scene.

Jared inwardly groaned. Why the hell hadn't he kept his hands to himself? Melissa's reputation was about to tumble over the falls and be washed down the Windy River. Why the hell hadn't he kept his hands to himself?

She was the first to speak. "It's not what you—"

But he cut her off. "I was inviting Melissa to join us for dinner," he told Stephanie, giving the two cowboys a warning glare.

"I knew it!" Stephanie beamed.

"The rain blew right in the windows," he went on, to

explain their appearance. Then he handed Melissa the hair clip. "Thanks for your help."

She gave him a puzzled expression. "There's no need—"

He stopped her with a stare. There was every need to protect her reputation, not to mention his own. She'd be gone in a week. In the meantime, he'd rather have the ranch staff think they were dating than carrying on a clandestine affair in the stable office.

He turned to his sister. "Did you need me for something?"

"Royce just called," said Stephanie. "He's at the airport."

"A day early?" That surprised Jared. He hoped nothing was wrong.

"And McQuestin called," Hal put in. "Some of the herd's still in the south canyon, and there's a risk of flooding down there."

"Hal and Barry are going to take half a dozen men," said Stephanie, but her goofy gaze was still on Melissa.

Jared knew he'd have to deal with his sister's letdown later. But at the moment, seeing the pure joy on Stephanie's face, he was inclined to wait until they got through the graveside visit on Sunday. He wondered if Melissa would be willing to go along with the charade. It would definitely distract Stephanie from missing their grandfather.

"Do you need me?" Jared asked Hal. He hadn't played cowboy in a few years, but he was ready and able if they needed an extra hand.

Hal shook his graying head. "Should be done by dark."

Jared gave the man a nod of acknowledgment. Then he looked at Stephanie. "I'll be right down."

She all but winked in return as she pulled the door shut.

"What are you *thinking?*" Melissa demanded as the footsteps receded down the hall.

"That you cared about your reputation." He stated the obvious.

"This isn't 1950."

"It's also not Vegas. It's Montana."

"People don't kiss in Montana?"

"They didn't know we were just kissing."

"But…" Melissa took a step back.

"Your lips," he told her softly. "Your hair, your clothes. You look like you just tumbled out of a haystack."

"But we didn't do anything."

"We thought about it," he told her gruffly. "And it shows."

Her glance went down to her chest. "Oh."

"Yeah. Oh."

Melissa swiftly pulled her hair to the base of her neck and fastened it with the clip. "What about Stephanie? You know what she's going to think."

Jared nodded. "I wanted to talk to you about that."

Melissa raised her brows.

"Would you mind playing along for a few days? Have dinner with us, pretend you like me, just enough to make Stephanie think there's a possibility we'll fall for each other."

Melissa seemed genuinely astonished. "Why? Why would you do that to your own sister?"

"You saw how excited she was," Jared pointed out.

"Yes. And I know how disappointed she's going to be when she finds out the truth. Not to mention how ticked off she's going to be at you."

"Who says she has to find out?"

"I'm leaving in a few days."

"That's perfect," he said. "It'll get us through Sunday. Then we'll act like it didn't work out. She'll be disappointed, sure. But she'll also be past the hard part of commemorating our parents' deaths and remembering how much she misses her grandfather."

"I don't think you can postpone grieving."

"Sure, you can." You could postpone it. You could ignore it. And you could replace it. With, for example, anger.

Melissa shook her head. "I'm not comfortable with this."

Then, he'd simply have to make her comfortable with it. "How much are we paying you?"

"Minimum wage, why?"

"I'll double it."

"You want me to ignore my principles and fake being your girlfriend for two times minimum wage?"

"Triple."

"Jared."

"Name your price."

"It's not about money. It's about integrity." For some reason her voice trailed away on the final word. Her gaze focused on the window as she watched the rain streak down the pane of glass. "Do you really think it's best for her?"

"I do." He moved up behind her. He couldn't help but admire Melissa's decision-making process. "Do you think you could pretend to like me?"

He saw her smile in the blurry reflection of the window. "I'm a pretty good liar."

"Good to know." He restrained himself from resting his hands on her shoulders, even though he longed to touch her again.

She turned, and his desire ramped up. "What do you want me to do?"

Jared bit his tongue over the loaded question, but his expression obviously gave him away.

"You." She poked him squarely in the chest. "Have to promise to behave yourself."

"I will. If you tell me what that means."

Her eyes narrowed. "It means…" She seemed to stumble. "It means not looking at me like you're the big bad wolf and I'm carrying a basket of goodies."

"It'll probably help the charade," he reasoned.

"It'll make me jumpy."

"It should," was his blunt answer.

"Jared," she warned.

"I'll behave myself," he promised. "But it'll help if you do a couple of things for me."

"What?"

"Wear a gunnysack, and a veil, don't talk in that

sexy voice and, for the love of God, quit smelling so decadently delicious."

Back inside her cottage, Melissa was all but shaking with reaction to Jared's words. And to his kisses. And to the overwhelming opportunity he'd unknowingly handed to her.

She was having dinner with his family. Dinner with the Ryders—a private meal where she could ask as many questions as she liked, about growing up, their ranch, their charity trust, their businesses.

She already knew the article would show them in a positive light. Both Jared and Stephanie were hardworking, successful people. The fact that they commemorated their parents' deaths was admirable, and their grandfather's recent death would add a poignancy that readers would lap up like kittens with fresh cream.

She lowered herself into the armchair beside the cottage window, struggling to frame her thoughts. It was Friday today. She'd planned to give herself one more day, maybe two at the most, to gather facts at the ranch. Then she'd have to rush back to Chicago and write the article in time to have it sitting on Seth Strickland's desk for Monday morning.

But that timetable was out the window now. Her greatest interview opportunities would be in the next couple of days. Which meant there was no way to be ready Monday morning. Which meant she'd have to call Seth and confess.

She drew a breath, squeezing the fabric-covered arms

of the chair as she tried to still her racing heart. She could only hope her editor's excitement over the article would overrule his anger that she'd lied to him.

She glanced at her watch. Two o'clock. That made it three in Chicago. No time to lose. She pulled her cell phone out of her bag, pressing the buttons for his number. It rang three times, but then jumped to voice mail, giving her no choice but to leave a quick, vague message.

She replaced the phone in her bag when, over the sound of the continuing rain, she heard footsteps on the front porch. She glanced through the window to see Stephanie, a dripping white Stetson pulled low on her head, waving cheerily through the pane.

Melissa sighed inwardly. She wasn't ready for this. Being undercover to get a story was one thing, but leading Stephanie on was another thing entirely.

But Stephanie had seen her, and Melissa had no choice but to open the door. She crossed to the little foyer.

"Hi," said Stephanie, beaming as she entered the cottage.

Melissa couldn't help but smile in return. The young woman's grin was infectious.

"I told you so," Stephanie sang, hanging her hat on one of a long row of pegs on the wooden wall.

The entry area of the cottage was practically laid out. There were pegs for coats and hats. A small bench beneath, with room for footwear under it, and a bright, woven Navajo rug decorating the wooden floor.

The foyer took up one corner of the small living

room. The rest of the room boasted a simple burgundy couch, a leather armchair, a small television and two low tables with ivory lamps.

There was a compact kitchen beside the living room, a table and two kitchen chairs under the front window, and a door to a bedroom/bathroom combination on the far side. Melissa had to admit, she adored the brass bed and the claw-foot tub. And the oak tree outside the bedroom window rustled in the night breeze, while the muted roar of the river outside filled in the background.

Melissa took a step back to stay out of the way of Stephanie's wet raincoat. Not that she wouldn't have to change clothes, anyway. Standing in front of the open window with Jared had been…well, it had been amazing, of course. But mostly it had been foolish. And not just because she'd ended up with wet clothes.

Stephanie kicked off her boots. "Do you know how long it's been since Jared invited a woman home for dinner?"

Melissa knew she needed to dial Stephanie's excitement level way down. "He didn't exactly—"

"Never," sang Stephanie. "He's never invited a woman home for dinner."

"Your equestrian center is not his actual home," cautioned Melissa. "And I was already here."

Stephanie waved a dismissive hand. "Technicalities."

"No. Facts."

Stephanie pouted.

"Seriously, Stephanie. You can't get carried away with this. Jared and I barely know each other."

Stephanie heaved an exaggerated sigh, dropping down onto the couch. "Are you always this much of a downer?"

Melissa took the armchair again. "I'm always this much of a realist."

"Where's the fun in that?"

"It saves a lot of heartache in the long run."

"Disappointment, I can handle. It's never leaving the starting gate that would kill me."

Inwardly, Melissa conceded there was some logic to the argument. "It's only dinner," she said to Stephanie. "And I'm still planning to leave in a couple of days."

"But you're here now," said Stephanie with a sly wink. "What are you going to wear?"

Melissa's cell phone jangled from her bag on the floor.

"I hadn't thought about it," she said, knowing in her heart the call was from Seth. There was no way in the world she could answer it in front of Stephanie.

It rang again.

"Do you want to get that?"

Melissa shook her head. "It can go to voice mail."

"You sure? I don't mind."

Another shrill ring.

"I'm sure. What do you think I should wear?" Truth was, Melissa hadn't seen anyone wear anything but blue jeans and riding clothes since she'd arrived. Her own wardrobe was plain and meager, since she was pretending to be on a bus trip.

The damn phone rang again.

"You sure you don't want to—"

"Completely sure." Melissa reached for the slim phone. A quick glance told her it was, indeed, her boss. She sent the call to voice mail. "There."

Stephanie paused for a moment. Then her expression grew animated once again as she sat forward. "I was thinking, since it's Royce's first night back, we should dress up a little."

Melissa's attention went automatically to the downpour and the rivulets of mud streaking the narrow cottage road. Even if she had brought anything dressy, it was a virtual mud bog between the cottage and Stephanie's house.

"We'll do it up at the house," Stephanie went on. "We're about the same size. You can take a shower up there. We'll play around with your hair. Put on a little makeup, and you can borrow one of my dresses. I have a bunch I've never even worn."

"I'm not Cinderella," Melissa admonished.

"Oh—" Stephanie all but jumped up from the sofa "—that makes me the fairy godmother."

"Did you miss the word *not?*" Melissa struggled to keep a grip on the conversation.

"This is going to be great."

Still in Melissa's hand, the phone rang again. It was Seth. She hit the voice mail button one more time. She was going to have one heck of a lot of explaining to do. Good thing she would have a kick-ass story to offer up.

"Girl talk while we get ready." Stephanie laughed.

Melissa paused.

Girl talk? *Girl talk.*

Why was she trying to get out of this? Girl talk was exactly what she needed for research.

"I'll meet you up there," she agreed. A quick call to Seth, and she'd be ready for all the girl talk in the world.

"Don't be silly." This time Stephanie did jump up. "You'd drown. I'll drive you over in the truck."

Stephanie's house was rustic but undeniably gracious. A large, practical foyer led into a massive great room with polished floors, a high, hewn-beam ceiling, and overstuffed leather furniture decorated with colorful pillows and woven throws. There was a huge stone fireplace at one end of the rectangular room, and a row of glass doors down the side opened onto a deck that overlooked evergreens and snowy mountain peaks. A wide passageway opposite revealed a gourmet kitchen with a long, polished-wood breakfast bar and padded stools and a formal dining room that seated twelve, with a wood-and-brass chandelier and an impressive woven carpet under the cherry table and wine-colored armchairs.

As they made their way up a wide staircase to the second floor, Melissa wished once again for Susan and her camera. Stephanie's bedroom was at the front of the house. It had its own small balcony, a walk-in closet, an en suite bath and a small sitting area set in a bay-window alcove.

"Dresses are way in the back," said Stephanie, flicking on the closet light and gesturing into the long room. "Pick anything you want. I'll hunt through the bathroom and see what I can find for makeup."

"What are you planning to wear?" Melissa gazed through the open door at rows of blazers and blouses, situated above open shelves that held blue jeans and jodhpurs. She stepped over several pairs of polished boots as she made her way across the carpeted floor.

Stephanie hadn't been exaggerating. There were at least two dozen dresses, most with the tags still on. They were black, gold, red, sleeveless, gauzy, and one gorgeous printed silk that shimmered gold and peach, with a jeweled scoop neckline that looked like something off a Paris runway.

"Try that one," came Stephanie's voice from the doorway.

Melissa shook her head. "I couldn't."

"Why not? Royce brought it back from Europe last year. The straps are too narrow for me. It makes me look like I have linebacker shoulders."

"It does not." Melissa laughed. Stephanie had a wonderful figure.

"I'm okay with sleeveless, even strapless, but there's something about those spaghetti straps that don't work. You want to hop in the shower? I put out fresh towels and a robe."

"I feel bad invading your privacy," Melissa said.

"Are you kidding? I can't wait to dress you up and wow my brother."

Melissa placed the dress back on the rack and turned. "I don't want you to get hurt," she told Stephanie honestly. "Jared and I barely know each other."

"You have to start somewhere," Stephanie replied, obviously undaunted by reality.

"The odds against he and I clicking are about a million to one."

"The odds against me winning Spruce Meadows last week were about a million to one."

"But you practiced. You worked hard for years and years to win that competition."

"I'm not expecting you to marry him next weekend."

Melissa took a step closer to Stephanie. "I'm not going to marry him at all. You have to understand that. He's a nice man. And maybe he thinks I'm pretty—"

"He's going to think you're a knockout in that silk dress."

Melissa sighed. "You're killing me here, Stephanie. I need to know *you* know this isn't going anywhere."

Some of the optimism went out of Stephanie's blue eyes. "But you're going to try, right?"

"It doesn't matter whether I try or not, the odds are still stacked way against it." And those odds were a whole lot higher than Melissa could admit.

"I'm not afraid of the odds," said Stephanie, a new equilibrium coming into her eyes. "I'm just leading a horse to water. He drinks or not will be up to him."

"I take it Jared's the horse?"

"And you're the water."

Relief poured through Melissa. Stephanie understood just fine. She wasn't some flighty young girl with impossible dreams. She was simply trying to match up her brother and bring some balance to the family's gender numbers.

The plan didn't have a hope in hell of working with Melissa, but she could respect the effort.

"Robe's on the door hook," said Stephanie. She nodded to the en suite. "Towels are stacked on the counter."

"Okay," Melissa agreed. She could play dress-up and ply Jared with questions. Maybe they'd have wine with dinner. Even better. She'd sip slowly and let his tongue loosen up.

She followed Stephanie's directions, enjoying the marble tub and the luxurious bath products. The towels were big and plush, and Stephanie's hair dryer gave Melissa's straight, blond hair some body and bounce.

She exited the room to find Stephanie sitting in front of her vanity in a white robe, her auburn hair damp around her ears.

Stephanie swiveled on the small stool. "What do you think?"

Melissa blinked at the unexpected sight. Stephanie's delicate features had been all but obliterated by glaringly bright makeup. With spiked lashes, bright blue shadow, dark blush and a fire engine–red lipstick shade, she looked ready for the lead in a 1980s disco flick.

"Uh...I..." Melissa struggled to find words.

Stephanie's face fell. "It's that bad?" She glanced back to the mirror.

Melissa rushed forward, reflexively putting her hands on Stephanie's shoulders. "The look's a little dated. That's all."

Stephanie hardened her jaw, glaring at her features. "Is it me? Do I just not have a feminine face?"

Melissa's jaw dropped open. "Are you kidding me?"

"I can never quite seem to pull it off." She gestured vaguely toward the closet. "It's not that I don't have the ingredients. I've got plenty of clothes, shoes, beauty products. But I can never figure out what to do with them. I bought a makeover magazine once. I ended up looking like a clown."

"You're beautiful." Melissa recovered her voice. "Beyond beautiful. You're stunning."

"I have a little-girl nose, ugly freckles and funny-color eyes." She leaned forward, screwing up her face in the mirror.

"Most women would kill for your nose," said Melissa honestly. "The freckles are pretty, and you just need a new shade of shadow." She turned the stool, looking critically at Stephanie's skin tone and features. "Go wash your face. Let's start over."

Stephanie perked up. "You'll help?"

"You bet I'll help."

Stephanie jumped up and headed for the bathroom, turning on the taps in the sink. "Did you have a mom and sisters and stuff?" she called.

"A mom, yes," said Melissa. "But I have five older brothers."

Stephanie popped her head back into the room. "Five?"

Melissa nodded. "Adam, Ben, Caleb, Dan and Eddy."

"So probably no makeup tips from them."

"Nah. But I can frame up a cabin, change a car's oil and whistle."

Stephanie laughed as she rubbed cleanser over her face. "And I can rope a calf in under thirty seconds."

"You never know when these skills might come in handy."

Stephanie rinsed and dried, walking back into the bedroom, clad in her terry robe. "Where did you learn about makeup?"

"Girlfriends at school, cable TV, demos at the mall." Melissa glanced around the room and realized the wide sill on the bay window was a good height.

"My friends were in the 4H club. And we didn't get many channels out here while I was growing up."

"Can you hop up there?" Melissa gestured. "That way I won't have to bend over."

"Sure." Stephanie held her robe as she got settled, her bare feet dangling.

Melissa selected some lotion and a few cosmetics and piled them on a small table in the alcove. "It's all about subtlety now," she explained, tipping Stephanie's chin toward the light. "Women want to look natural, just a little more beautiful than nature intended. Earth tones will bring out the subtle silver in your eyes, instead of clashing with it."

"Can you cover up my freckles?"

Personally Melissa liked the freckles. "I'll tone them down a bit. They'll be less noticeable. You have amazing skin."

"Fresh air and healthy living."

"It works. I'm in an office all day, air-conditioning and recycled smog."

Stephanie's forehead wrinkled. "You have a job?"

"I used to have a job." Melissa cursed inwardly at her stupidity, struggling to recover from the gaff. "I delivered office mail for a while. Very boring."

"You seem so smart."

"I'm not that smart."

"Jared said you knew about Sierra Benito."

"That was a stroke of luck." Melissa found a thin brush and some powdered, charcoal eyeliner. "I happened to read an article in the newspaper."

"But you remembered it."

"I suppose. Close your eyes."

"You must have a good memory."

"Decent." Memory was a critical attribute for a journalist—names, dates, faces, events. Melissa gently stroked on the liner, chose silver, blue and pale purple for shadow, added a subtle blush and finished off with a neutral lip gloss.

Then she found a comb and piled Stephanie's thick, wavy hair in a loose twist at the top of her head, freeing a few locks to frame her face and trail at the back of her neck.

Melissa stood back. "Go take a look."

Obviously self-conscious and nervous, Stephanie hopped down from the ledge. She gingerly crossed the floor to the mirror, squinted, opened her eyes, then stared in silence.

"Wow," she finally breathed, turning her head from side to side. "I'm gorgeous."

"You certainly are."

Stephanie raised her brows to Melissa, mischief lurking in her silver-blue eyes. "Let's do you."

Seven

It wasn't often Jared saw his little sister dressed to accentuate her femininity. Not that he ever forgot she was feminine, but she'd run around the ranch yard like a tomboy ever since he could remember. So tonight when she waltzed into the great room in an ultra-flirty dress, he was momentarily stunned. It was white on top, with bows at the shoulders and a full black skirt that billowed around her knees. She'd done something with her hair, too. And her face looked—

Melissa appeared from behind Stephanie, and the jolt took his breath away. Where Stephanie was feminine, Melissa was sultry. She wore a shimmering thin silk sheath of a dress that clung to her figure like a second skin. Spaghetti straps adorned her smooth shoulders, while the gold and peach shimmered under the warm light. Her hair was upswept, her face flawless, and her long, tanned legs and spiked heels were going to invade his dreams for at least the next year.

He swallowed.

"Is Royce here yet?" asked Stephanie.

When Jared finally dragged his gaze from Melissa, he saw the twinkle in Stephanie's eyes. He had to hand it to his sister, she knew how to matchmake. Nothing would happen between him and Melissa, but it sure wouldn't be from a lack of desire. Given his own way, he'd drag her off to his bed right now.

"Sunset Hill flooded out," he answered. He'd talked to Royce a few minutes ago, and his brother had decided to wait the storm out at the main house with McQuestin.

Fine with Jared.

He didn't particularly want Royce laying eyes on Melissa, anyway.

Stephanie's lips pursed in a pout. "Why doesn't he ride up?"

"Probably because he'd be soaked to the ass in the first half mile." Jared gave a quick glance at Melissa to see if his coarse language had offended her.

Her little grin was the last thing he saw before the room went black.

Forks of lightning streaked through the thick sky, while thunder cracked and raindrops smashed against the roof and the wooden deck outside.

"Uh-oh," came Stephanie's disembodied voice.

"What happened?" asked Melissa.

"Could have been anything," Jared answered as he made his way toward the mantelpiece. He found a box of matches by feel, struck one and lit a couple of candles. Power outages were common in ranch country, doubly so during storms.

Stephanie crossed to the front window. "I don't see the cookhouse," she said.

"Give it a minute," Jared suggested, flipping open his cell phone. He punched in Royce's number.

Melissa joined Stephanie at the window, and Jared let himself enjoy the view of her back.

"Why would you see the cookhouse?" asked Melissa.

"They have an emergency generator," said Stephanie.

"Hey, bro," came Royce's voice on the phone.

"Lights out down there?" asked Jared.

"Just now."

"Us, too. Any problems?"

"The boys aren't back from the canyon yet," said Royce.

"McQuestin worried?"

"Won't be for a couple more hours."

"Keep me posted?"

Melissa turned, and Jared quickly averted his lecherous gaze.

"Sure," said Royce.

Flickering lights came on in the distance.

"Cookhouse is up," said Jared, and Melissa turned back to the window.

"We're striking up the gas barbecue," said Royce.

"Don't let McQuestin talk you into poker."

Royce laughed as he signed off.

Stephanie had moved into the dining room. She was on her own cell phone, checking to make sure the employees were all accounted for.

Jared tucked his phone in his pocket.

"What now?" asked Melissa.

He checked to make sure Stephanie was out of earshot as he moved toward Melissa and the window. He kept his voice low. "Now I tell you you're gorgeous."

"Stephanie's idea."

"My sister's not stupid."

"Your sister is Machiavellian."

He moved his hand forward and brushed Melissa's fingertips. "Seems a shame to let her down."

"Seems a shame to lead her on."

"Hey, she's the one playing us, remember?"

"Mrs. Belmont left lasagna in the oven," came Stephanie's voice.

Jared reflexively backed off.

"Salad's in the fridge," Stephanie finished.

"I guess we're dining by candlelight," said Melissa.

"Romantic," Stephanie put in, scooping one of the lighted candles and heading for the dining room.

Melissa followed.

Jared allowed himself a lingering glance at Melissa as she walked away. "Better than poker with McQuestin," he said out loud.

They settled at one end of the big table, Jared at the head, flanked by the two women. Lasagna, salad, rolls and a bottle of merlot were spread out in front of them. He'd lit a candelabra for the middle of the table, and kerosene lamps flickered against the rain-streaked windows.

Melissa's soft blond hair shimmered in the yellow light. Her lips were dark. Her eyes sparkled. And the silk shifted softly against her body as she moved her hands.

"Do you have political aspirations?" she asked him.

The question took him by surprise. "Why the heck would you think that?"

"You've got it all," she responded, taking another sip of the merlot, which he couldn't help but note was exactly the same shade as her lips. "Money, success, community standing, charitable work, and now you're palling around with the mayor of Chicago."

"How did you know about the mayor?"

She concentrated on setting down her glass. "One of the cowboys mentioned something about your building and the city."

Jared turned to glare at Stephanie. "How does anybody get any work done around here?" he demanded. "Melissa's been here three days, and she knows everything but my birth weight and shoe size."

"Don't be such a bear," said Stephanie.

"You're exaggerating," said Melissa.

"Not by much."

"Eight pounds nine ounces," Stephanie put in with a giggle.

"Ouch," said Melissa.

"Don't let that put you off," Stephanie came back. "It's not necessarily hereditary."

Both Jared and Melissa stared at her, dumb-founded.

"What?" Stephanie glanced back and forth between them. "You guys don't want kids?"

"Several," said Jared, deciding his sister deserved everything she got from here on in.

He took Melissa's hand and raised it to his lips. "How does four sound to you?"

"Are you going to hire me a nanny?" she asked, surprising him by playing along.

"You bet. A nanny, a chauffeur and a housekeeper."

"Okay, then." Melissa gave a nod. "Four it is. But we'd better get started—I'm not getting any younger." She reached for her wineglass. "Better enjoy this while I can. Once I'm pregnant, it's off the alcohol. And this wine is fantastic."

"I know you're messing with me," Stephanie put in. "But I don't care. I have hope, anyway."

"We have a very good wine cellar," said Jared. "It was a hobby of Gramps."

"Why don't you show it to Melissa?" Stephanie quickly suggested.

"You hoping I'll get her pregnant on the tasting table?"

Melissa sputtered and coughed over a drink.

He squeezed her hand by way of apology.

"I think Stephanie's overestimating the power of this dress," she wheezed.

Jared hesitated. Then he stepped into the breach. "No, she's not."

Stephanie clapped her hands together in triumph.

* * *

It was ten o'clock when Stephanie succeeded in getting Jared and Melissa alone together. They were in the truck, and Melissa peered in pitch-darkness and driving rain as they rounded the bend to the row of cottages by the river, the headlights bouncing off the oak trees and the dark porches.

She had to admit, she wouldn't have wanted to walk all the way back. And she wouldn't have asked Stephanie to slog through the mud to get to the truck. And that left Jared.

Then he had insisted on carrying her from the ranch house porch to the truck—which was an experience all on its own.

Now they pulled up to the front of her cottage and he killed the lights and turned off the engine.

"Stay put," he told her as he opened the driver's door and a puff of cool wind burst in. "I'll be right around."

Part of her wanted to insist on walking, but her shoes were impractical, the mud was slick, and she knew the black road would be a patchwork of deep puddles. So she waited, her heart rate increasing, her skin prickling in anticipation and her brain fumbling through sexy projections of being in Jared's arms again.

Her door swung open, and she shifted from the seat into his arms, wrapping her own arms around his neck. She'd put a windbreaker over the dress, but her legs were still bare and his strong hand clasped around the back of her thigh.

"Ready?" he asked, husky voice puffing against her cheek.

"Ready," she confirmed with a nod, and he pulled her against his chest, his body protecting her from the worst of the rain. He kicked the truck door shut and strode over the mud and up the porch stairs, stopping under the tiny roof in front of the door.

He didn't bother putting her down. Instead, he swung the door open and carried her into the warm cottage.

It was completely dark, not a single frame of reference.

He slowly lowered her to the floor. "Don't move."

"Do you have matches?" she asked as he stepped away from her.

"There'll be some on the mantel." Something banged, and he cursed.

"You okay?" she called.

"I'm fine."

Then she heard a crackle, and a small flame appeared across the living room. She could just make out Jared's face as he lit three candles on the stone mantel. There was a mirror on the wall behind, and the light reflected back into the room.

"Thanks," she told him.

He shook out the match and tossed it into the fireplace. "You want a fire?"

"It's not that cold." She hung the damp windbreaker on a wall hook. Then she wiped her face, pulled the clip from her hair and finger-combed out the rainwater.

It was late enough that she planned to snuggle into bed with her laptop and record notes from the evening.

Stephanie had predicted the power would be back on by morning. If not, the staff would gather at the cookhouse for breakfast, and they'd set priorities for animal care.

Jared crumpled up a newspaper, threw it into the fireplace and added a handful of kindling. "It's not that warm, either." He crouched down and struck another match, lighting a corner of the newspaper.

The orange flame quickly grew, reflecting off the planes and angles of his face. There was something about the actions that warmed Melissa's heart. He hadn't exactly saved her life, but he'd shown a tender, caring side that surprised her.

She automatically moved closer to the fire. "I wish I could offer you coffee or something."

He rose to his feet in the flickering light. His short hair was damp, and his cotton shirt was plastered to his chest. Power and masculinity seemed to ooze from every pore.

He eased closer, and she was instantly awash in desire.

"Coffee's not what I want."

She was dying to ask, but she didn't dare. She opened her mouth, then closed it again, warning herself that the slightest encouragement was going to bring his lips crashing down on hers, and they'd be trapped all over again in the tangle of desire.

His lips came down on hers, anyway.

And she might have stretched up slightly to meet him.

Okay, she'd definitely stretched up. And she'd tilted her head to accommodate him. And now she was opening her mouth, meeting his tongue, snaking her arms around his neck and pressing her body tightly against his own.

His clothes were damp, but she didn't care. His hands were roaming, and she loved it. His mouth was sure and strong, but still tender, and oh, so hot.

Passion quickly obliterated reason. She clung tightly as his nimble hands pulled down the zipper of her dress. He eased it over her head and discarded it on a chair. He worked at the buttons of his shirt, alternating between kissing her and staring deeply into her eyes. His were nearly black with passion, while desire pulsed through every fiber of her body.

Her hands went to his jeans, popping the button, sliding the zipper.

He groaned, tossed his shirt and pulled her back into his arms. His kisses roamed her cheeks, her neck and down to where he pushed her bra out of the way. His hot mouth surrounded a nipple, and she threw her head back, her hands grasping his shoulders for support.

He wrapped a strong arm firmly around the small of her back, holding her steady, his mouth sending sparks of desire from her breasts to the base of her belly. He released her bra, dropping it to the floor. Then he scooped her into his arms and carried her to the small bedroom.

The sheets were cool against her bare back. She could barely make out his outline as he discarded the remainder of his clothes. Then his warm, hard, musk-scented body was sliding next to her, and she was enveloped in kisses and caresses that seared heat over every inch of her skin.

She kissed his chest, tasting his salty skin, her hands roaming down his back, over his buttocks, along his strong thighs.

He groaned his approval, kissing her deeply. "You are gorgeous," he breathed. He kissed her again. His fingers found their way into her flimsy panties.

She gasped at his touch, flexing her hips, transmitting an unmistakable invitation.

He peeled off her panties, produced a condom from somewhere, and covered her body with his own. Their bodies were flush together, tight at the apex, and her legs were wrapped around his waist.

He kissed her deeply, sliding his hands to her bottom, adjusting the angle of their bodies as he eased inside. Driving rain splattered against the bedroom window. Lightning chased across the sky while thunder vibrated the cottage walls.

Then the world around Melissa disappeared. Nothing existed beyond Jared, and every sensation was magnified a thousand times, his touch, his scent, the taste of his skin, the sound of his voice as he recited her name, calling her beautiful, urging her on.

Their tempo increased. The hot and cold and electric sensations heightening to unbearable. As thunder crashed around them, her body stiffened. Her toes curled. Her hoarse voice cried out Jared's name as she tumbled from the pinnacle down into the exquisite arms of release.

As she floated to earth, Jared tucked a quilt around

them. He turned slightly to the side, keeping them locked together, but taking his weight from her body.

Their deep breaths rose in unison, both of them sucking the moisture-laden oxygen from the dark room, recovering, reframing, realizing the magnitude of what they'd just done.

"I'm not sure that was such a good idea," she ventured on a gasp.

He didn't let her go. Didn't back off a single inch. "Because you work for me?" he mumbled against her neck.

Because I'm writing an article on you. Because you don't know who I am. Because I lied to you. The reasons were endless, and she couldn't admit to any of them.

"At least for tonight," she ventured, instead, "do you think we could be clear that I work for Stephanie?"

Jared's chuckle rumbled through his frame. "So what's the problem?"

"I'm leaving in a few days."

He smoothed her hair from her forehead. "Just because something's short, doesn't mean it can't be fantastic."

"I suppose." If you took away her deception, a one-night stand certainly wasn't the end of the world. But eventually he was going to find out her true identity.

She couldn't do anything to change the past hour, but she did need to control herself going forward. Not that she'd *ever* divulge any intimate details. Every single thing that happened in the cottage tonight was off the record.

But she did need to back off. She couldn't let their circumstances get even more complicated.

She eased away from his warmth. "Stephanie's probably counting the minutes you've been down here."

"Are you asking me to leave?"

"I think that would be best."

He stilled, and she assumed he was staring at her in the dark.

A lightning bolt lit up the room, and his stark expression of disappointment tugged at her heart.

"I think it would be best," she repeated, wanting nothing more than to burrow down under the covers and sleep in Jared's warm arms for the rest of the night. But she had to be strong.

He rolled from the bed. "Of course." There was a tightness to his voice that bordered on anger.

She closed her ears to it and clung to the passion they'd shared.

His jeans rustled. Then he padded into the living room.

She held her breath while he dressed. Would he come back? Say something more? Kiss her goodbye?

Suddenly his silhouette appeared in the doorway. "Good night," he offered without coming back inside.

"Good night," she echoed, struggling to keep the hollowness from her voice. She'd asked him to leave. She was silly to feel hurt.

He waited a moment more, then turned away, heading out into the storm.

The truck engine rumbled to life. The headlights

flared up. Then the big treaded tires churned their way over the muddy road.

Melissa dragged herself from the bed. She wrapped a robe around her body, retrieved her laptop, powered it up and forced her thoughts back to the discussion at dinner. The fling with Jared might be over, but she still had her job to save.

"Seth Strickland," came the terse answer at the other end of the phone.

It was morning. The rain had stopped, and the lights were back on as Stephanie had predicted. Melissa was dressed in blue jeans and a simple tank top again, trying to push the insanity that had become her life back into perspective.

"Seth?" she said into the phone, thanking her lucky stars that he was in the office on a Saturday. "It's Melissa."

"Where the hell have you been?" he shouted without preamble.

She wasn't ready to answer that question yet. "If I could *guarantee* the Jared Ryder story, can you buy me a little time?"

"No! And what the hell are you talking about? Why didn't you call me back yesterday?"

"I'm in Montana."

"You said you were working from home."

"I'm at the Ryder Ranch. Right now. I had dinner with Jared Ryder last night."

Seth went silent.

"I need a few more days, Seth."

"You had dinner with Ryder?"

"And his sister. And his brother's just arrived."

"How the hell did you—"

"They think I'm a stable hand."

"You're undercover?" There was a note of respect in Seth's voice. "It's an exposé?"

"Yes, I'm undercover."

"What've you got?"

"A bunch of stuff. His family. His childhood. Their charitable foundation."

"Ryder has a charitable foundation?"

"Yes. But I need a few more days. Can you give it to me?"

"You're in a position to guarantee the story?"

"Yes."

There was a long silence. "If I go to Everett and you don't deliver, you know both our asses will be out the door."

"I understand."

"And you can still make the guarantee?"

"I can." She didn't have enough on the construction business yet. But she'd let Stephanie matchmake some more, and she'd find a way to meet Royce. She'd get what Seth needed or die trying.

"I have to have it Wednesday. Five o'clock. And the copy better be bloody clean. We're not going to have time for much editing."

"Five o'clock Wednesday," Melissa confirmed.

"And, Melissa?" Seth's voice was gruff.

"Yes?"

"Lie to me again, and you're fired."

"Yes, sir."

Seth hung up the phone, and she realized she was shaking. The stakes couldn't be higher, and she barely had four days to pull it off.

"Have a good time with Melissa last night?" Stephanie asked as Royce's pickup appeared in the distance on the ranch road.

"It was fine," Jared answered, keeping his voice neutral. He fully expected Melissa to make herself scarce for the rest of the week.

He wasn't sure what had gone wrong at the end of the evening, but he'd obviously made some kind of misstep. A woman didn't go from crying out a man's name to kicking him out of her bed in the space of two minutes if the guy hadn't screwed up somehow.

He started down the stairs to meet Royce at the driveway.

"You going to see her again?" asked Stephanie, keeping pace.

"I expect I will. Since she's living here." Odds were that he'd run into her eventually.

"That's not what I meant. Are you going to ask her out? I noticed you stayed down there for a while."

"I bet you did."

The sound of the truck's engine grew louder. Mud sprayed out from the tires as Royce took a corner far too fast.

"Did you sleep with her?" asked Stephanie.

Jared shot his sister a glare of irritation. "What is the matter with you?"

She shrugged. "You were only gone an hour. Not a lot of time, but then maybe you weren't very—"

"Young lady, you shut your mouth before you get yourself into a world of trouble. Where did you learn to talk like that, anyway?" Maybe he'd stayed away too long. Maybe leaving Stephanie here on her own was a mistake. Or maybe Gramps's death had affected her more than Jared and Royce had realized.

"I'm just asking a question."

"You're out of line, little sister."

Stephanie pursed her lips in a pout. "So are you going to ask her out again?"

Jared frowned.

"That can't be out of line. I'm not asking about sex."

The truck skidded to a halt, and Jared walked forward. "Let's just get through the weekend, all right?"

"I know I have to get through the weekend," Stephanie muttered as they walked down the front pathway. "I was only hoping for something to look forward to at the end of it."

Jared felt a pang of guilt. The whole reason he'd started the charade with Melissa was to keep Stephanie's mind occupied. Sure, it had run way off the rails last night. But that wasn't Stephanie's fault.

He slung an arm around his sister's shoulders, moderating his voice. "Fine. I'll ask her out again. But I can't guarantee she'll say yes."

Stephanie turned in to give him a tight squeeze. "I know she'll say yes. I saw the way she looked at you."

The words caused a sudden tightening in Jared's

chest. How she'd looked at him? What did that mean? He wanted to probe for more information. But Royce appeared across the hood of the truck, and Stephanie broke free to hug her other brother.

"Baby sister!" cried Royce, dragging Stephanie into his arms, lifting her off the ground and twirling her around.

Jared caught a glimpse of Melissa across the yard, and their gazes met. She was shoveling manure again, and for some reason, that made him angry. She was capable of so much more. She was intelligent, full of insightful opinions and thought-provoking questions.

It occurred to him that he could offer her a job in Chicago. She could work for Ryder International or even the Genevieve Fund. There had to be any number of things a woman with her intellect and curiosity could handle.

In a split second he realized what he was doing. He was working out ways to keep her close, ways that he could see her again, maybe sleep with her again. Though, judging by the expression on her face, the latter was unlikely. But what did it say about him? Was he buying into Stephanie's fantasy?

He could almost feel a debate going on inside Melissa's brain. She'd seen him, and she knew he knew. Did she duck her head and go back to work? Did she avoid him, or get the first, awkward moment over with?

While he waited, she squared her shoulders, leaned the manure fork against the fence and determinedly marched toward him. Good for her. He couldn't help a surge of admiration, and he moved to meet her in the driveway.

"Melissa!" Stephanie's voice surprised him. "Come and meet Royce." Hand in Royce's, Stephanie tugged him to intersect Melissa's pathway. The four of them met up off the hood of the truck.

"Royce, this is Melissa," said Stephanie. "She's dating Jared."

Melissa's eyes widened slightly, but she held her composure.

Royce turned to stare at Jared.

Jared gave his brother an almost imperceptible shake, and Royce immediately held out his hand to Melissa. "Great to meet you. I'm the black sheep of the family."

Stephanie laughed, while Melissa accepted Royce's handshake. "Melissa Webster. I'm the black sheep in mine."

"She has five older brothers," Stephanie put in.

"Worse off than you," Royce teased, arching a brow at his sister.

"I'd better get back to work," said Melissa. Her gaze darted to Jared just long enough to let him know she wished they'd been able to talk. Well, so did he. He felt like he owed her an apology of some kind. At the very least, he wanted to make sure things were okay between them.

"Can you come and help me with Rosie-Jo?" Stephanie asked Melissa.

Since Rosie-Jo had half a dozen grooms, Jared recognized the ruse for what it was. Stephanie wanted to

pump Melissa for information. But from what he'd seen
of Melissa so far, she'd be up to the task of sidestepping
anything too personal.

"Dating?" Royce asked as the two women walked
away.

"More like flirting," said Jared. "But I didn't have
the heart to disillusion Stephanie this weekend."

"Are you going to disillusion poor Melissa?"

Jared shook his head. "She knows the score. She's
leaving in a few days, anyway."

Royce reached into the back of the pickup truck
and retrieved his duffel bag. "How's Stephanie holding
up?"

"Too cheerful," said Jared. "You just know she's
going to crack."

"Maybe going up to the cemetery isn't such a good
idea this year. Gramps's grave is awfully fresh."

"Go ahead and suggest we skip," said Jared as the two
men headed for the house. Quite frankly, Jared would
rather avoid the cemetery. He wanted to pay tribute to
his grandfather, but the anger at his parents hadn't abated
one bit. His whole life, he'd admired and respected them
both, never doubting their morals and integrity. But he
couldn't have been more wrong. He wanted to yell at
them, not lay flowers beside their headstones.

But he couldn't let on. Bad enough that he knew
the truth. He couldn't drag Royce, and certainly not
Stephanie, into the nightmare. At the moment, he wished
his grandfather had taken the knowledge to his grave.

"She'd never go for it," said Royce, yanking Jared
back to the present.

"Of course not," Jared agreed as they crossed the porch. Stephanie considered herself tough. She'd never admit how much visiting the cemetery hurt her.

"I hear there's a debate over Sierra Benito." Royce tossed his duffel on a low bench in Stephanie's foyer.

"There is. You're the deciding vote."

"You going to try talking me out of the project?"

"I am. I don't want another death on my conscience." An image of Jared's father sprang to his mind. There was no excuse. No excuse in the world for what his father had done.

Royce paused and peered at his brother. "*Another* death?"

"Slip of the tongue," said Jared, turning away to move into the great room. "I don't want anyone to die on a Ryder project."

He also didn't want to keep lying to his brother, about his parents, about Melissa, about *anything*.

Eight

Under the small light above the cottage's kitchen table, Melissa typed furiously on her laptop. She'd composed and discarded at least five openings to her article. She knew if she could get the beginning right, the rest would flow. It was always that way.

But she needed to capture Jared's essence. No small feat. Every time she thought she had him pegged he'd show her another side of himself, and she'd have to rethink the package.

Maybe it would be easier if they hadn't made love. Maybe if she hadn't seen him naked, or gazed into the depths of his eyes, or felt the strength and tenderness of his caress.

She drew a frustrated sigh as the words on the screen blurred in front of her. Unless she wanted to sell the article to a tabloid, she was going to have to nix that train of thought.

Someone tapped lightly on her front door.

The sigh turned into a frown. It was Sunday night, and the two young women staying next door had invited her over for drinks. The two had seemed very friendly, but Melissa had begged off. Between her ranch chores and allowing for time to fly back to Chicago, she only had two more evenings to pull the article together. There wasn't any time for socializing.

The knock came again.

With the light on, there was no sense in pretending she was asleep. Besides, they would have seen her through the window on their way up the stairs.

She pushed back from the table and crossed to the door.

"I'm sorry," she began as she tugged it open. "But I really can't—"

"Sorry to bother you," came Jared's voice.

His broad shoulders filled the doorway. His head was bare, and he still wore his business suit from the cemetery visit earlier. He wore a crisp, white shirt and a dark, red-striped tie. There was a frown on his face and worry in his eyes.

"Jared."

"I was out walking and I saw your light," he apologized.

Even if she had been inclined to give up a chance to get more information, his expression would have melted the hardest heart. She knew he'd been up to the cemetery with his sister and brother this afternoon, and it had obviously been tough.

"How did it go?" she asked, stepping back to invite him in.

He shrugged as he walked inside. "About how I'd expected." His voice was hollow. "We all miss Gramps."

Melissa nodded, closing the door behind him. "This is probably the worst year," she ventured.

"I suppose." His gaze focused on something, and she realized he was staring at her laptop. "You travel with a computer?"

Panic spurred her forward. She closed the lid, hoping she'd saved recently. "It's compact," she answered. "Very light."

"I guess. Did I interrupt—" he paused "—work?"

"I'm writing a letter," she quickly improvised. "Can I offer you something? Coffee?" She gestured to the small living-room grouping, taking his attention away from the table and her computer. "Or there's a bottle of wine…"

"I'm fine." He eased down into the worn armchair.

Melissa curled into one corner of the sofa, sitting at right angles to him. "How's Stephanie doing?"

"She's asleep now."

Melissa nodded. She was starting to feel close to Stephanie. The woman was fun-loving and generous. She wasn't exactly worldly wise, but she was perfectly intelligent and worked harder than anyone Melissa had ever met.

"I wish there was something I could do to help."

Jared gazed at her without speaking, an indefinable expression on his face. It was guarded, yet intimate, aloof, yet intense.

"Tell me what you were writing," he finally said.

Melissa could feel the blood drain from her face. The air suddenly left the room, and an oppressive heat wafted over her entire body.

"A letter," she rasped.

"To who?" he asked.

"My brother," she improvised, dreading what Jared must know, hoping against hope for a miracle.

"Which one?"

She waited for his eyes to flare with anger, but they stayed frighteningly calm.

"Adam." She swallowed. "I promised...I promised him...that I'd, uh, be careful."

Jared nodded. "And have you? Been careful."

"Yes."

He raked both hands through his short hair. "Oh, God, Melissa. I don't want to do this."

She jumped up from her chair, too nervous to sit still, sweat popping out of her pores. "Do what?"

"It's so unfair to you."

What was he talking about? What was he planning to do to her? She found herself inching toward the door, wondering if the women next door were still awake. Would they hear her if she screamed?

"I didn't know where else to go." His voice was suddenly thick with emotion.

The tone made Melissa pause. "What do you mean?"

Was he going to yell at her? Toss her out of the cottage? Throw her off the property?

She was starting to wish he'd just get it over with. Should she try to grab the laptop?

He shook his head. "Never mind."

Never mind?

He came to his feet, and she struggled not to shrink away.

"Did you say something about wine?" he asked.

She gave herself a mental shake, struggling to clear her brain.

"Melissa?"

"Are you angry with me?"

"Why would I be angry with you? I'm the one invading your privacy." A beat went by. "And attempting to drink your wine."

She forced herself to move. "Right. It's on the counter." What had she missed? What had just happened?

She heard him moving behind her as she opened a wooden drawer. "I think I saw a corkscrew in here."

"It's a screw top."

"Oh." Classy. She was willing to bet he didn't often drink wine from a screw-top bottle. "One of the cowboys picked it up in town," she explained.

"Did you have to flirt with him?"

"For screw-top wine? Please."

Jared grinned. "I forgot. I'm talking to the master."

"I gave him ten bucks and told him to do the best he could." She hunted through the cupboard, but gave up on wineglasses. "These do?" At least they weren't plastic.

"You sure you should be spending your hard-earned money on wine?" he asked. He poured while she held the glasses.

"You tripled my wages, remember?"

"Did we agree on that?"

"We sure did."

He set down the bottle, taking one of the short water glasses from her hand. "Get it in writing?"

"Didn't have to." She gave him a mock toast. "I know your secret."

"No, you don't," he responded dryly, downing a good measure of the wine.

She watched his stark expression with a whole lot of curiosity. Jared had a secret? Something other than playacting for his sister?

Okay, it couldn't be as big as Melissa's secret. But it might be interesting. And it could be exactly the hook she was looking for to get the story started.

Jared hadn't meant his words to sound like a challenge. But he realized they did. And if the expression on Melissa's face was anything to go by, she'd reacted the same way.

"So?" She sidled up to him, green eyes dancing with mischief.

"None of your business."

"Then why'd you bring it up?"

Fair question. Better question, why was he even here? It had been one roller coaster of an emotional day. He'd been half blind with anger at the cemetery, holding on to his temper by a thread, knowing he couldn't let Stephanie or Royce catch on.

He could tell Royce was suspicious. So when Stephanie went upstairs to bed, Jared had escaped from the house. Then he'd seen Melissa's light, and his feet had carried him to her door.

He thought he knew why. He needed to spend time with someone completely separate from his family. Melissa didn't know any of the players in their little drama. She knew nothing about his family but what he'd told her. She might annoy him or argue with him or frustrate the hell out of him with her approach to life, but she wouldn't threaten his composure.

She grazed her knuckles along his biceps. "You said you had a secret?" she prompted.

Here was another reason to darken her doorway. Her musical voice soothed him. Her scent enticed him. And when he gazed at her lips, all he could think about was capturing them with his own, tasting her all over again and letting the softness of her body pull him, once more, into oblivion.

And maybe it was as simple as that. He'd come to her because he needed to forget for a while.

He captured her hand, holding it tight against his sleeve, the warmth of her palm seeping through to his skin.

"I want you," he told her honestly.

Her voice went husky, stoking his desire. "That's not exactly a secret."

He smiled at her open acceptance of his declaration.

He liked it that she wasn't coy. She was confident and feisty. She flouted convention, ignored advice. There was something to be said for a woman who marched to her own drummer.

"I was expecting something more interesting," she said.

"Like what?"

"I don't know. A secret takeover of a multinational corporation. News that Ryder International was sending a manned mission to Mars. Maybe that you were really a CIA agent masquerading as a businessman."

Jared couldn't help but laugh at the last one. The knot of tension in his gut broke free. "The CIA?"

"Didn't you read the article?"

"What article?"

"In the *Chicago Daily*. Two years ago. Well, they outed you as a spy in the lifestyle section. Though, I suppose if they'd had any real evidence, it would have made the front page."

"You remember what you read in the *Chicago Daily* two years ago, yet you can't remember how to tie a quick-release knot?"

"Are we still talking about sex?"

"You're amazing." He'd never met anyone remotely like Melissa. She was smart, sassy and stunningly gorgeous. How had the men of Gary, Indiana, let her get away?

"So you're not in the CIA?" she pressed with a pretty pout.

He slipped an arm around her waist, settling her close and letting the balm of her company soothe him.

A breeze wafted in over the river, fluttering the plaid curtains above the small sink. The lights were low, the evening cool, the woman beautiful.

"You caught me," he said, setting his glass on the countertop and sliding hers from her fingers. "Ever slept with a spy?"

"You'd lie to get me into bed?"

"Is it working?"

"I'm not that impressed by a spy. I'd rather you were an astronaut going to Mars."

He settled his other arm around her waist, squaring her in front of him. "I can be anything you want."

He kissed her, gently, savoring her essence, forcing himself to keep it short. It was a struggle. If he let his hormones have their way, he'd be scooping her into his arms and tossing her on the bed all over again. But he pulled back.

"Is this why you came here?" Her cheeks were flushed, her lips parted and soft, but her eyes were slightly wary.

He felt like a heel. "No pressure," he quickly told her.

"Is it because I'm leaving?"

"Yes," he answered honestly. Then he realized how that sounded. "No. That's not it." He cursed himself for stumbling. "Well, it's partly…"

What was the matter with him? "I like that you don't know me, don't know my family." He wrapped his hand around the back of a kitchen chair, giving it a squeeze. "It's been a rough day."

She moved forward. "I understand."

She didn't, but it didn't matter. What mattered was that the wariness was out of her eyes. What mattered was that she was touching him, drawing forward, stretching up to kiss his lips.

There was something unfair about the situation, something unbalanced, unequal, but he couldn't put his finger on it. A split second later, he didn't even want to try.

His arms went firmly around her. He wanted to pull her inside him, keep her there, cradle her while the world moved on without them.

Her arms snaked around his neck. She tipped her head, and he deepened the kiss. Her tongue was sweet nectar, the inside of her mouth hot and decadent. She smelled like wildflowers and tasted like honey.

His hands slipped down, cupping the softness of her bottom, kneading and pressing her against his driving arousal.

She moaned his name, and he felt her breasts burning into his chest, like a brand that would mark him forever.

He lifted her, shoving the chair out of the way, perching her on the table, tugging the curtain shut behind her, before his hands went to the buttons on her shirt.

She reciprocated, her breath coming fast, head down to concentrate as she worked on his long row of buttons.

He freed her shirt, slipping it off her shoulders, kissing the velvet softness, letting his tongue explore the taste and texture of her skin. He snapped open her bra, and it fell to the floor, revealing firm, pert breasts, capped with pink nipples.

She pushed his shirt down his arms, and they were skin to skin. She was impossibly soft, impossibly warm, silken and sweet and everything a man could possibly dream.

Their lips came together, open, full on. He led her through a tumultuous kiss that left them both panting and needy for more. He kissed her again while he slid his palm up her rib cage to cover her breast, testing the hardened nipple, drawing a gasp from the back of her throat.

He caressed her body, leisurely, thoroughly; while her own hands splayed on his back, her lips found his flat nipples, and her silken hair teased his skin with an erotic brush. He scooted her forward, forcing her thighs farther apart. His fingers went to her blue jeans, releasing the button, sliding down the zipper. His knuckles grazed her silken panties, and his mind fixated on the treasures beneath.

A gust of wind cooled his back. The crisp scent of the river and the sweet aroma of the fields swirled through the room. The moon rode high above the mountains, while layers of stars twinkled across the endless sky. Horses whinnied in the distance, while leaves rustled in the oak and aspen trees.

There was perfection in the world tonight. He was home and she was in his arms, and nothing else mattered for the moment. Tomorrow would have to take care of itself.

He tugged off her jeans, then slipped off her panties,

drawing her exquisite, naked body against him for a long lingering kiss.

He finally drew back, gazing down at her ivory skin, unblemished against the scarred wood of the kitchen table.

"You are stunning," he whispered with reverence.

"You're overdressed," she said back, her hand going to his waistband.

He closed his eyes, tipped his head back and let his body drink in the erotic sensations as she slowly dragged down his zipper, her smooth warm hands removing his pants, releasing his body, highjacking every molecule of his senses.

"You're stunning, too," she whispered, body wriggling, hand moving, sliding, squeezing.

He sucked in a tight breath, holding on to his control as he feathered his hand along her thighs. He stared into her bottomless eyes. She stared back as his fingertips climbed higher, and her hands roamed further, each of them daring the other to crack.

Her beautiful mouth parted. Her eyes glazed. Her hand convulsed, and he pulled her to him, slipping slowly, surely, solidly inside.

She gripped his shoulders and leaned in for his kiss. He melded his mouth to hers, slipped his hands beneath her and settled the angle, settled the rhythm, let the roar in his ears and the pounding in his brain obliterate everything but the incredible sensation of Melissa.

He wanted it to go on forever. He was determined to make it last. She finally cried out, body pulsating before going limp. But he kept on kissing her, muttering words of need and affection.

And then she was with him. All over again, building toward a second crescendo. And he held back until the very last second before allowing himself to tumble over the cliff with her, his body drenched with sweat, his mind filled with amazement.

He carried her spent body to the bed, climbing in beside her, settling the quilt around them as he drew her into the cradle of his arms.

"You okay?" he whispered as his head found the indent on her pillow.

She drew two deep breaths while he kissed her hairline, then her temple, then her ear. He burrowed into the crook of her neck, inhaling deeply. How could a woman possibly smell so good?

"Define okay," she whispered back.

"Still breathing?"

She nodded.

"Nothing strained or broken?"

"Nothing."

"Want to do it again?"

An hour later Melissa could barely lift a finger. But she could see why Jared was the fantasy of half the women in Chicago. Word had obviously gotten around.

She was lying on her back, eyes closed. The covers were a tangle at their feet, and a cool breeze relieved her heated skin. Jared was beside her, propped up on one elbow, his fingertips feathering a small zigzag pattern over her stomach. She was amazed he could move anything.

"You still breathing?" he rumbled.

"Barely."

He chuckled at that.

"I don't think I've ever been this exhausted," she said.

"Never?" There was a hint of pride in his voice.

"Well, maybe once," she couldn't help teasing. "The day my brothers decided to build a tree fort. I was eight and insisted on helping. They nearly killed me."

"You're saying I'm a close second to your brothers?" The pride was gone.

She opened her eyes and managed a grin.

"Still feisty," he said.

"Even when I'm beat."

"Tell me about these burly construction-worker brothers of yours."

"What do you want to know?"

"If they'll have my name on a hit list when I get back to Chicago."

"If I was eighteen you might be in trouble."

"If you were eighteen, I wouldn't be in this bed."

She chuckled. "But they've mellowed over the years. Caleb wouldn't hurt a fly. Eddy's head over heels for a kindergarten teacher right now. He doesn't even call anymore. Adam, Ben and Dan are married with little kids and more important things to worry about than their sister's virtue."

"It's strange to hear all that," said Jared. "I keep picturing you as an orphan. How does such a big family let you wander off on the bus system without money? It doesn't make sense."

"It's my pride. I don't talk to them about money."

"Still, if it was Stephanie—"

"What about you?" Naked in Jared's arms, Melissa really wasn't in the mood to have to lie to him. "Extended family? Niece and nephew prospects?"

"No niece and nephew prospects. Stephanie's too young, and Royce...well, you haven't had a lot of time to spend with Royce. It's hard to picture him with a wife and a white picket fence."

"And you? Do you really want four kids?"

"I like kids," said Jared. "But I wonder..."

"It's not like you can't afford them," she put in. And he'd certainly have his pick of women. She could give him a list right now if he was interested.

His hand stilled on her stomach. "Money isn't everything."

"Said like a man who has plenty."

"There's love, affection, fidelity."

"Fidelity?" she questioned.

He didn't respond.

"Aren't you getting a little ahead of yourself?" she asked. He might want to marry the lucky woman before he planned the divorce.

Jared shifted. "It's not a given."

She tipped her head so that she was looking at his face. "Maybe. But you don't go into something planning for failure, either."

He was gazing through the open window at the near-full moon. "You can love each other, or appear to love each other, and your marriage can still crumble."

"You're a cynic."

"I'm a realist."

A sudden unease came over her. "Jared? Have you been divorced?"

He shook his head. "No."

But she could tell there was more. She waited as long minutes ticked by.

"What's wrong?" she finally asked.

Tension radiated in waves from his body.

"Jared?"

"My mother was unfaithful."

The admission hit Melissa with the subtlety of a brick wall. She was too shocked to speak.

"The old cabin," Jared rasped. "That bedroom." His hand raked through his messy hair. "Until I saw it, I'd hoped Gramps's memory had somehow…"

Melissa's stomach clenched around nothing. "Oh, Jared."

He met her gaze, his irises dark with the depth of his pain. "My whole life, I thought their deaths were an accident."

"They weren't?" Melissa struggled to understand what he was saying.

"My grandfather told me. Before he died. I guess he thought…" Jared drew a ragged breath. "I don't know what he thought. I wish he hadn't told me at all."

"Somebody killed your parents?"

"My mother's affair started a chain reaction, and three people ended up dead."

"Three?" Melissa squeaked.

Jared's tone turned warning. "Stephanie and Royce don't know. I have to pretend everything is normal."

Melissa nodded her understanding. "You went to the graveyard to keep the secret."

"Yes."

And he'd come to her afterward. She had no idea how she should feel about that.

He suddenly pulled her close, his face getting lost in the length of her hair, his arms and legs imprisoning her against his body.

"It's stupid," he told her. "I barely know you. But when I think of another man…" Jared drew another breath. "For a second tonight, I understood why my father shot him."

Melissa reflexively stiffened. "Your father shot your mother's lover?"

"Yes."

She swallowed a sickening feeling. "And the man died?"

"Yes. And that same night my parents' truck went off the cliff. But my grandfather didn't know that. So he threw the gun in the river. Two accidental deaths and a homicide with no clues. Nobody ever made the connection. *I* never made the connection."

Melissa's heart went out to Jared. What an incredible burden. And he was bearing it all alone.

"You should tell Stephanie and Royce," she advised.

Jared scoffed out a cold laugh. "Why?"

"They could help you cope."

"I'll be fine." His voice grew stronger. "Today was the worst. It'll get easier now." He gave a sharp nod. "I'll be fine."

Melissa wasn't so sure. "Do you think maybe they deserve to know?"

"Nobody deserves to know this."

She wasn't going to argue further. She barely knew the family. Who was she to give them advice?

"I wish I could stay here," he said.

"Me, too." She'd like nothing better than to sleep in Jared's arms. The morning might be awkward, but at the moment she was willing to risk it.

His hug loosened. "I leave for Chicago tomorrow afternoon."

"Oh." She thought he was talking about staying the night. But he meant he was leaving the ranch. She backed off, slightly embarrassed by her presumption. She forcibly lightened her tone. "Of course. I know you have a big company to run."

"Come with me."

"Huh?"

"Come to Chicago. I have a Genevieve Fund event Tuesday night. We could go together. Spend a couple of nights in the city. Afterward, I'll buy you a plane ticket to Seattle. You'll be right back on schedule with your trip, and you won't have to worry about the bus."

Nine

There were a dozen reasons Melissa should have said no. Not the least of which was Stephanie's resultant excitement and Royce's knowing grin. There was also Melissa's deception and the article and, though she hated to admit it, the very real possibility she was falling for Jared.

She glanced at his profile across the aisle in the compact private jet. Royce was in the pilot's seat, while the two cream-colored, leather seats facing Melissa and Jared were empty. Four others behind them remained empty, as well.

Jared had offered her a drink and snacks after takeoff, but her stomach was too jumpy for either. Was she crazy? What if there were press at the charitable event? What if somebody recognized her?

As the jet began its descent, Jared reached across the aisle for her hand. "The ball's at the Ritz-Carlton, so I booked us a suite. Royce is staying in my apartment."

Melissa nodded. She'd have loved to see Jared's apartment, but she understood he wanted them to be alone. And so did she. She wanted a night with him to herself—no Stephanie up the hill, no ranch hands next door and definitely no Royce in the neighboring bedroom.

Maybe heartache would hit her afterward. And she might be weeks recovering. But she knew a stolen fling with Jared would be worth it.

"You have a spa appointment tomorrow," he continued. "And we can wander down North Michigan Avenue and find you a dress."

"You know how to spoil a girl." She had several perfectly acceptable dresses at home, but she couldn't admit that to Jared.

She felt another twinge of guilt over the deception. But it would end soon. And Jared might never read the article. Even if he did, he'd have to be pleased with it, she told herself. She intended to show him in a very good light.

His gaze was warm. "I'll spoil you for as long as you want."

"You don't need to spoil me at all." She brought his broad hand to her lips. "What I want from you is free."

"I'd rather give it to you at the Ritz-Carlton."

She affected a deep sassy drawl. "You can give it to me anywhere you like, cowboy."

He pursed his lips and hissed a drawn-out exclamation. "I sure hope Royce plans to entertain himself after we land."

"What are you doing now?" Stephanie's voice came through Jared's cell phone while he sat in a comfortable armchair by the window in St. Jacques boutique overlooking the lake.

"Watching Melissa try on dresses." He'd made three overseas calls and consulted with his finance department while Melissa had paraded past in about a dozen dresses. She looked great in them all.

"I bet she looks gorgeous."

"She does."

Melissa walked out of the changing room in a short gold sheath with spaghetti straps and a diaphanous scarf. He wasn't crazy about the scarf, but he liked the dress.

He held up four fingers. He'd been giving rankings out of five, since he'd been holding his PDA to his ear through the entire fashion show.

Melissa leaned forward and pointed to a looped gold-and-diamond necklace the salesclerk had fastened around her neck. He simply gave a thumbs-up to that.

"Did you have fun last night?" Stephanie asked.

"None of your business."

"It's quiet here. I miss you and Royce."

"We miss you, too. Come to the party. Royce will pick you up."

"I can't." She sighed. "We've got our first junior elite

rider starting tomorrow. He's been blowing them away on the young rider circuit."

"That's a good thing, right?"

"It's a great thing."

"Then quit your whining."

Melissa pranced back into the changing room, and he wished he'd thought to comment on the shoes. Black, sleek and high, with flashing rhinestones around the ankles. He definitely wanted her to keep the shoes.

"Is this tough love?" Stephanie asked.

"Absolutely."

"What's going on with Melissa?"

"She's going to blow them away tonight."

"Will she blow you away?"

"Don't get your hopes up, Steph."

"You have to fall in love sometime."

"Not necessarily."

But then Melissa appeared again. This time she was wearing an emerald-green strapless party dress. The bodice was tight satin, stretched snugly over her breasts, while the skirt puffed out around her thighs, showing off her toned calves and sexy ankles. It was perfect for a late-night club. It was also dress number thirteen, and he realized he wanted to take her out in all of them.

"Gotta go," he said to Stephanie, needing to end the conversation.

"Keep an open mind," she called into the phone.

"Don't worry." No point in Stephanie worrying. Jared was the one who needed to worry.

He was starting to think about jobs for Melissa again, jobs at Ryder International. Or better still, jobs at affiliated companies in the city, so she wouldn't work directly for him. But she'd still be around to date him.

He was starting to think about her skill set and who owed him favors. They had one more night together, then maybe half of tomorrow. But he knew that wasn't going to do it for him. And that was a very worrisome development.

"She's a knockout," came Royce's voice as he dropped into the armchair beside Jared.

"No kidding."

Melissa gave Royce a welcoming smile and a little wave.

Royce's long lecherous look at her legs irritated Jared, worrying him all over again. Just how deep had he let himself fall?

"You serious about her?" Royce asked.

"Why?" Jared demanded, wondering what might have given him away.

Royce gave a smug grin. "Guess that answers my question."

"She leaves for Seattle tomorrow." And that was the disappointing truth. He'd suggested she stay longer, but she'd insisted she had to get back on her trip. Whatever feelings might be building inside Jared, this was the time to shut them down.

"You want me to fly her out?"

"No." Jared did *not*. He might not be pursuing anything with Melissa himself, but that didn't mean the field was open to his brother.

Royce's grin widened. "This is fun."

"Back off."

"Not a chance."

Melissa floated out in a calf-length ivory gown. It had snug, three-quarter-length, flat lace sleeves and a sweetheart neckline gathered with a line of jewels at mid-bust. There was a wide ribbon waist band and a two-layered, flowing skirt that flirted with her legs. She grinned and gave a twirl. Her diamond earrings twinkled under the bright lights.

Jared felt a tightening in his chest. A small bouquet of flowers, and she'd be the perfect bride. Her open smile told him she was oblivious to the image, but he wasn't, and he drank in the sight for several long minutes.

He gave the dress a five, and she turned to walk away.

"Do I need to say it?" asked Royce.

"No." Jared kept his focus on Melissa until she disappeared again.

"So how're you going to keep her here?"

Jared gave up lying both to himself and to Royce. "I haven't decided yet."

They'd chosen a black silk dress with spaghetti straps and a metallic gold thread that made it shimmer under the ballroom lights. The skirt of the dress was full enough to make Melissa feel like a princess as she whirled around the dance floor in Jared's arms to the music of a five-piece string band. Her rhinestone sandals were light on her feet. Her hair was upswept, and Jared had insisted on buying her the looped gold necklace and a set of matching earrings.

He looked roguishly sexy in his tuxedo. Having seen

him in blue jeans, chaps and dust, she realized the formal clothes barely disguised the rugged man inside.

Champagne flowed, and the crystal chandeliers glittered around them as they moved past marble pillars, magnificent floral arrangements and the kaleidoscope of designer gowns. At one point, the mayor paused to chat. And everyone in the room knew and obviously respected Jared.

Though Melissa had promised herself the night was off the record, she'd decided to use a few of her impressions in the article. Jared was an intelligent, insightful man, with an amazing grasp of local issues and Chicago economic trends. There was no way she could leave that side of him out of the article.

Though she'd spent the first hour with an eagle eye out for press and anybody else who might recognize her, it turned out to be a private party. No press, and Jared's social circle was far from hers. While she might recognize the notable figures from their pictures and television appearances, she knew they'd never recognize her.

She felt like Cinderella when they finally made their way out of the ballroom and into the promenade. Her arm was linked with Jared's, and Royce was by their side.

"Barry left them at the front desk," Royce was saying, thumbing a button on his PDA before he tucked it back into his breast pocket.

"I don't want to work tonight," said Jared, and he raised Melissa's hand to his lips, giving her knuckles a tender kiss.

Royce sent Melissa a mock frown. "See what you've done? *I'm* usually the irresponsible brother."

"Not tonight," said Jared.

"Apparently not," Royce growled.

"Is it important?" asked Melissa. She was anxious to get Jared alone in their suite, but his conversations at the ball had taught her his time was valuable. His business interests were even more significant and far-reaching than she'd realized.

"Yes," said Royce.

"No," Jared put in over top of his brother.

"Do you want to get up early, instead?" asked Royce.

"No," Melissa quickly put in. She'd have to pretend to get on a plane to Seattle sometime tomorrow, but she'd been entertaining a glorious vision. One that featured a leisurely breakfast in bed with Jared, maybe a dip in their whirlpool tub and a long goodbye before they went their separate ways at, say, noon.

"Just sign them," said Royce. "I'll go over them with Barry before I countersign."

"Who's Barry?" asked Melissa.

"Ryder's financial VP," said Jared, and she could feel his hesitation.

"I don't mind waiting," she quickly put in as they stepped into an open elevator.

Royce quirked his brows at Jared, and Jared gave a nod. He pressed the button for the lobby. The door closed, and the car *whooshed* smoothly down twelve floors.

"I won't be long," Jared assured her, hand resting

lightly on the small of her back as they stepped into the opulent lobby.

She gestured toward the far side of the huge room. "I'll check out the paintings while I wait."

He nodded, and left with Royce for the front desk.

It wasn't much of a hardship to wander through the lobby. Marble walkways, elegant, French-provincial furnishings, magnificent sculpture and glorious flowers combined with the soft lighting to create a serene ambiance. It wasn't the kind of hotel where Melissa normally stayed. Then again, this wasn't exactly the kind of week she usually experienced, either.

Her heels clicked as she rounded the fountain, moving toward the main glass doors. There were a couple of furniture groupings that looked inviting. Her new shoes were comfortable, but the heels were high, and her calves were beginning to tighten up. A gold armchair beckoned. It would give her a nice view of the front desk. She could people-watch, while keeping an eye out for Jared.

But then she spotted a man on the sidewalk and halted in her tracks. He was in profile, smoking a cigarette in the muted light outside, but it was definitely Brandon Langard.

Melissa gasped, then whirled around before he could spot her. The rest of a lobby blurred in front of her panicked eyes.

"Melissa?" Her coworker Susan Alaric suddenly appeared in front of her. "*Melissa?* Oh, my God. You're back. How'd it go?"

Melissa opened her mouth to speak, but only a squeak emerged.

Susan's face nearly split with an excited grin. "Seth said you got on the ranch. Did you get the interview? Did Ryder figure out who you were?" She tipped her head back in glee. "Oh, man, Brandon is going to have a cow."

Melissa grasped Susan's arm. "Susan…" she rasped, but then her gaze caught Jared's face over Susan's shoulder, and her stomach roiled.

"The *Bizz* is going to have the scoop of the year," Susan finished.

"The *Bizz*?" Jared's voice and eyes both darkened to thunder.

Susan heard his voice and took in Melissa's stricken expression. She twisted around to look at Jared. Then she swallowed. She opened her mouth, but gave up before she could find any words.

Royce appeared, taking in the trio. He noted Susan's camera, then paused on his brother's expression. "What the hell?"

"Jared…" Melissa began, mind scrambling with panic.

She'd explain it was a good article. It would focus on the most complimentary things. He was successful, hardworking and kind. And his family was wonderful. It wasn't like they had any skeletons in their closets.

Okay, so there *was* the thing with his grandfather, but that wasn't relevant, and she sure wasn't going to write about that. And everything that had happened between them was way off the record. This wasn't a tabloid tell-all. It was a serious journalistic piece.

But before she could pull her thoughts together, his hand closed over her arm and he pulled her away from Susan and Royce.

"You *lied* to me." His graveled voice was harsh in her ear.

She didn't answer.

"You're a reporter?" he demanded.

She closed her eyes, but then forced herself to nod the admission.

"And *I'm* your subject."

"Yes, but—"

"You are going to walk out that door." He stopped, jerking her to face him. His words were measured, but she was subjected to the full glare of his anger. "You are going to walk out that door. You are going to do it quickly and quietly, and I *never* want to see you again."

"But—"

"Do you understand me?"

"I'm not going—"

"Do you understand me?"

She closed her mouth and nodded, chest tight, throat closing in. She told herself he'd read the article. Eventually he'd know she hadn't betrayed him.

"Good." He flicked his hand from her arm, his eyes filled with contempt.

She had to try one more time. "Jared, please let me explain."

"You already have. I know who you are. And I know what you've got."

"I'm not going to—"

"Know this," he cut her off, leaning in, lowering his voice to steel. "If you do *anything* to harm my family, I will destroy you."

Then he turned away, sharply and with an absolute finality to his posture.

Before she could get another word out, he was past the fountain and heading for the elevators.

"Melissa?" Susan's voice was hushed as she pressed against her shoulder.

"That was Jared Ryder." Melissa's voice was hollow. Her body was hollow. Her life was hollow.

"No kidding."

Melissa knew it didn't matter what she wrote in the article, what secrets she kept or what she revealed, Jared was never going to forgive her. She'd never see him again, never be held in those strong arms, hear his voice, smell his skin, taste his passionate kisses. She realized now how very much she'd been counting on their last night together.

"You okay?" asked Susan.

Melissa forced herself to nod. Her eyes were burning, but she blinked the sting away.

"Wow," Susan continued. "I hope your research was finished."

Melissa didn't know whether to laugh or cry. Just then, she couldn't have cared less about the article. "It is," she told Susan.

"What are you doing here?" Susan glanced around

the hotel lobby. "Brandon and I were hoping to catch the mayor."

Melissa coughed a hollow laugh. "I chatted with the mayor upstairs."

"Really?" Susan took in the dress. "You were at the Genevieve Memorial Fund ball?"

"Jared and, uh, his brother invited me along." The last thing in the world she wanted to do was invite questions about her relationship with Jared.

"Wow," said Susan, gaze going to the elevator where the two men had disappeared. "I am in awe."

Where Melissa was exhausted, both emotionally and physically. It had been a week of hard work and long nights. She'd labored over the article every spare minute. Well, every spare minute that she hadn't been falling—

She froze for a second, drew a stunned breath and closed her eyes.

Every spare minute that she hadn't been *falling in love with Jared*.

Her hands curled into fists, and she fought against the knowledge that had just exploded in her brain.

"Your article is going to kick butt," Susan was saying.

How could Melissa have been so stupid? Why hadn't she seen it coming? She should have done something to stop it. But no, she'd hung around him like an eager little puppy dog, throwing herself into his arms, into his bed, pretending she somehow belonged in his life.

Susan squeezed Melissa's shoulder. "You are *so* going to get that promotion. Seth might even smile." She paused. "Hey, Brandon's outside. You think we should go tell him?"

"*No.*" The word jumped out with more force than she'd intended. But Melissa didn't want to talk to Brandon or anyone else. She wanted to go home and hole up alone in her apartment. Some way, somehow, she had to get over Jared and get words on the page in the next twenty-four hours.

"You slept with a reporter?" Royce confirmed the obvious as the hotel-suite door swung shut behind them.

The fact that Jared had slept with Melissa was the least of his worries. Sure, maybe she could write about seeing him naked or detail his kisses and pillow talk. But it wasn't like he was into handcuffs or women in French-maid outfits.

"You didn't suspect?" Royce went straight for the bar, snagging a bottle of single malt from the mirrored top shelf.

He flipped two crystal glasses over, ignored the ice bucket and filled the tumblers to halfway.

"Yeah," said Jared. "I suspected. But I figured, what the hell? She's got a great ass. Why not sleep with somebody who'll splash it all over the front page?"

Royce rounded the bar again. "Sarcasm's not going to help."

"Neither are stupid questions." Jared took one of the glasses and downed a hefty swallow.

"Nothing gave her away?"

Jared dropped into an armchair. "She was a stable

hand. We have dozens of them. Yeah, she didn't know much about horses. And maybe her background was vague. And maybe she seemed too smart for a drifter. Which was what attracted me in the first place. She was…"

Royce cocked his head meaningfully.

"Son of a bitch," said Jared and polished off the scotch.

He'd let his sex drive override his logic. It was a clichéd, blatant, pathetic scenario. And he'd bought it hook, line and sinker. "She slept with me to get a story."

"That surprises you?"

Yes. It surprised him. He knew there were women in the world who used sex as a bargaining chip. He met them all the time. But Melissa sure hadn't struck him as one of those. She was down-to-earth, honest, classy.

"She told me she had brothers." Jared coughed out a flat chuckle. "I was afraid they might come after me."

"For defiling their sister?"

"I think about Stephanie sometimes…"

Royce stood and picked up the empty glasses. "Someday, some guy's going to sleep with Stephanie."

"He better be in love with her."

"He'd better be married to her." Royce poured a refill for each of them. This time, he added ice, then he wandered back to the opposite armchair.

"So what does she know?" he asked.

Jared slouched back, loosening his tie and flicking his top shirt button open. "The ranch, Stephanie's jumping, you, Anthony, the Genevieve Fund."

"What you look like naked," Royce put in.

Jared waved a dismissive hand. "It's not like we took pictures."

"Good to know."

Jared gazed out the wide window, letting his vision go soft on the city lights. He'd expected the night to turn out very differently. Even now, even knowing Melissa was a traitor, on some level he wished she was lying in the king-size bed, sexy, naked, waiting for him to join her.

"What's she got?" Royce asked quietly.

Jared blinked his attention back to his brother.

He had to tell him. There was no way around it.

He'd been colossally stupid to share it with a perfect stranger.

"Gramps," he said. Then he tugged off his tie, tossing it on the table.

Royce's eyes narrowed.

"He told me something. Right before he died." Jared drew a breath. "He told me Dad killed Frank Stanton."

The room went completely silent.

Jared dared to flick a glance at Royce.

His brother was still, eyes unblinking, hands loose on the padded arms of the chair. "I know."

Jared drew back. "What?"

Royce took a sip of his drink. "I've always known."

Jared took a second to process the information. Royce knew? He'd kept silent all these years?

"I don't understand," said Jared.

Royce came to his feet, then carried his drink across

the room, turning when he came to the window. "The day it happened. The day they died. I found a letter Mom had written to Dad. It was half-finished. It said she loved Frank. It said she was leaving Dad. She was leaving us." He took another sip.

"You didn't *tell* me?"

His brother was silent for a long moment. "You know, sometimes, when you *have* to keep a secret? The only person who can know is you. The second—" he snapped his fingers "—the second you let that knowledge out of your brain, you put it at risk. I knew that. Even at thirteen years old."

Jared couldn't believe his brother hadn't trusted him. "I would never have—"

"Our father was a murderer. Our mother was unfaithful. And Stephanie was two years old."

"You should have—"

"No. I shouldn't have. I didn't. And I was right." Royce paused. "I didn't know Gramps knew."

"He threw the gun in the river," said Jared.

Royce gave a half smile. "Good for him."

"He got rid of the gun before they found Mom and Dad. He thought Dad would go on trial for murder."

"Yeah." Royce returned to his chair. "Well, what do you do? He protected his son. Who are we to decide how far a man goes?"

"Do you kill your wife's lover?" The question had been nagging at Jared for weeks now. He couldn't help picturing Melissa. And he couldn't stop the cold rage that boiled up inside him at the thought of another man.

"I don't have a wife," said Royce. "I don't have to make that decision."

Jared nodded. "Simpler that way."

"It is," Royce agreed. He sat back down. "Do we tell Stephanie?"

Jared hated the thought of hurting his sister. But if the story came out in the article, she needed to be prepared. He hoped it wouldn't come to that, but he feared it might.

"Not yet," he answered Royce.

The *Bizz* was a monthly magazine. He'd have at least a few days to think about solutions.

So far, all he'd come up with was a plan to kidnap Melissa and lock her up in a tower in Tasmania or Madagascar with no telephone or Internet. Unfortunately his mind kept putting himself in the tower with her, in a big bed, where they'd make love until he tired of her. Which, if his wayward imagination was anything to go by, would take a very, very long time.

Ten

From the moment Melissa clicked the send button, she feared she'd made a mistake. While she certainly had the legal right to file her story on Jared, she wasn't so sure she had the moral right to do it.

Then she'd tossed and turned all night long, imagining his anger, his reaction, Stephanie's thoughts and feelings when she found out Melissa had been a fraud. Melissa was going to get a promotion out of this, no doubt about it. Seth was nearly beside himself with glee. Brandon was surly and sulking. And Everett himself had sent her an e-mail congratulating her on the coup.

Susan had guessed she was feeling guilty. But in her usual pragmatic style, she'd advised Melissa to put it behind her and focus on her future. Jared was a big boy, and he'd get over the inroad on his precious privacy.

It was a positive article. The quotes Melissa had used were accurate. She hadn't made anybody look foolish or mean-spirited. She'd mentioned Stephanie's jumping trophies, Jared's hardworking ancestors, his move from cattle ranching to construction to save the family's land. And she'd made Royce look like a fun-loving maverick. He'd probably get a dozen marriage proposals out of the coverage.

She hadn't used a single thing she'd learned from sleeping with Jared. Still, she couldn't shake the feeling she was wrong.

It lasted through her morning shower, through the breakfast she couldn't bring herself to eat, during the train ride to the office in the morning, up the elevator to her floor and then all the way to her desk.

Jared was an intensely private man. She'd invaded his privacy on false pretenses. And even though she hadn't used their pillow talk in her article, she'd crossed a line. She'd befriended him. She'd gained his trust. She'd let him think he could let his guard down, and he had.

Plus, and here was the crux of the matter, she'd fallen in love with him. And you didn't betray the person you loved. You were loyal, no matter what the circumstances, no matter what was to be gained or lost. You were loyal.

That was why Jared's grandfather hid the gun. An extreme example, perhaps. But his loyalty was to his son, and he'd risked his freedom to protect him. Melissa wouldn't even give up a promotion.

She dropped her purse on her desk, her gaze going to Seth's office. His head was bent over his desk—no doubt

he was working his way through her article. It would go
upstairs by lunchtime, be typeset by the end of the day
and move along the pipe to the printing press.

At that point, nothing could stop it from hitting the
streets. She had one chance and one chance only to make
things right. Jared might not love her, and he might never
speak to her again. But she loved him, and she had to
live with herself after today.

She crossed the floor to Seth's office, opening the
door without knocking.

He jerked his head up. "What?"

"I've changed my mind," she said without preamble,
striding to his desk.

His mouth dropped open in confusion.

"The article," she clarified. "You can't run it."

Seth's mouth worked for a second before it warmed
up to actual words. "Is this a joke? It's not funny. Now
get the hell out of my office. I have work to do."

"I'm not joking."

"Neither am I. Get out."

"Jared Ryder does not want us to print it."

"Jared Ryder can stuff it. We need the numbers."

Melissa began to panic. "You can't run it."

"Yes, I can."

She scrambled for a solution. "I lied, Seth," she lied
baldly. "I made it up. The quotes are bogus, and I was
never on the Ryder Ranch."

Seth's complexion went ruddy, and a vein popped out
in his forehead. "Have you gone insane?"

"I'll swear to it, Seth. I'll tell the whole world I made
up the story."

"And I'll fire your ass."

"I don't care!" she shouted. She had to stop him. She couldn't let her work see the light of day.

Seth's gaze shifted to a point over her left shoulder and his eyes went wide.

Fear churned in her stomach, but she carried on, anyway. It was her last chance to make things right. "If you run it, I'll swear I made the whole piece up. The *Bizz* will get sued, and *you'll* lose *your* job."

Seth's mouth worked, but no sound came out.

"Don't test me on this, Seth," she vowed. "Pull the article. I'll quit. I'll go away quietly. You can make up whatever you want to tell Everett."

"Noble of you," came a voice behind her.

Everett. The publisher had heard her threats.

Not that she'd expected to keep her job, anyway, but it was humiliating to have an additional witness. She clamped her jaw, squared her shoulders and headed for the door.

Her stomach instantly turned to a block of ice.

In the doorway next to Everett stood Jared. They both stared at her, faces devoid of expression.

Neither of them said a word as she forced one foot in front of the other. She prayed they'd step aside and give her room to get out the door.

They did, but inches before freedom, Jared put a hand on her arm. Neither of them looked at the other, and his voice was gruff. "Why'd you pull the story?"

She struggled with the cascade of conflicting emotions that swamped her body. She was proud of herself.

She was brokenhearted. She was frightened and unem-
ployed and exhausted.

She decided she owed him her honesty. So she
glanced up and forced the words out. "The same reason
your grandfather did what he did."

Love. Plain and simple. When you loved someone,
you protected them, even at a risk to yourself.

Then she jerked away, grabbed her purse from her
desk and kept right on going to the elevator.

Jared's first impression of Seth Strickland was hardly
positive, so he didn't much care now that the man looked
like he was going to wet his pants. Seth had shouted at
Melissa. And while he was shouting, it was all Jared
could do not to wring his pudgy little neck.

Jared might be angry with her, but that didn't give
anyone else license to hurt her. Sure, she'd betrayed him.
But she was fundamentally a decent person. Even now,
he was battling the urge to chase after her. Not that he
knew what he'd say. Not that he even understood what
had just happened.

She'd behaved in a completely incomprehensible
manner. Of course, she'd baffled him from the moment
they met.

While Jared struggled to put her in context, Everett
stepped into the office, moved to one side, then gestured
for Jared to enter.

Everett shut the door firmly behind them and focused
on the sweating Seth Strickland. "Mr. Ryder, this is Seth
Strickland, *Windy City Bizz*'s managing editor. For now.

Seth, this is Mr. Jared Ryder, the new owner of *Windy City Bizz.*"

Seth's jaw dropped a notch further.

Jared didn't bother with pleasantries. It seemed a little ridiculous after what they'd just witnessed.

"Is this a copy of the article?" He advanced on Seth's desk and pointed to the papers piled in front of him.

Seth nodded.

"We won't be running it," said Jared, lifting the pages from under Seth's nose.

He gave Everett a polite smile. "Thank you for your time. One of Ryder International's vice presidents will be in touch next week."

Then he turned and exited the office. He couldn't care less if Everett fired Seth or kept him on. Melissa wasn't fired, that was for sure. And she could write for Seth or for anyone else in the company.

He took the elevator to the first floor, crossed the lobby, trotted down the outside stairs and slid into the Aston Martin idling at the curb.

"How'd it go?" asked Royce, pushing the car into gear and flipping on his signal.

"It's taken care of," said Jared.

"Good." Royce gave a nod. Hard rock was blaring on the stereo, while the air conditioner battled the heat from the sunshine.

"Did you see Melissa come out the door?"

Royce zipped into the steady stream of traffic. "You saw Melissa?"

"She was inside." Jared shoved his sunglasses onto the bridge of his nose.

"And?"

"And." Jared drummed his fingers on the dashboard. "She was trying to get her editor to kill the article."

Royce glanced at him for a split second before turning his attention to the busy intersection. "What? Why?"

"Beats the hell out of me. The guy fired her."

"She lost her job?"

"No. Of course she didn't lose her job. She works for us now, remember?"

"And you don't think *we* should fire her?"

Jared killed the clanging music. He needed to think.

"Jared?" Royce prompted.

"Why would she kill the article?" Her cryptic remark about his grandfather didn't make sense.

"Maybe she's afraid of getting sued."

Jared glanced down at the papers in his hand. He scanned one page, then another, then another. The story was innocuous. It was lightweight to the point of being boring.

"Anything about Gramps?" asked Royce as they turned to parallel the lakeshore. Skyscrapers loomed to one side, blocking the sun.

"Nothing. It's crap."

"She's a bad writer?"

"No. She's a fine writer. But she held back. She had a ton of stuff on me." He flipped through the pages again. "She didn't use any of it."

"Then why did she try to pull it?"

"I asked her," Jared admitted, flashing back to that moment, remembering her expression, remembering the emotional body slam of seeing her again, his desire to attack Seth and to chase after Melissa.

"Bro?" Royce prompted.

Jared cleared his throat. "She said it was the same reason Gramps did what he did."

Royce's hand came down on the steering wheel. "All this, and the woman's talking in riddles?"

Jared rolled it over in his mind. "Why did Gramps do what he did?"

"To protect Dad."

"Why?"

"Because he was his son."

"And…"

The brothers looked at each other, sharing an instant of comprehension. Gramps had protected Jared's father because he loved him.

"Holy crap," said Royce.

"*Not* what I needed to know," said Jared.

"Do you care?" Royce pressed.

Jared swore out loud. "She lied to me. She duped me. She invaded the hell out of my privacy." He slammed the pages onto his lap.

"Yet you love her, anyway," Royce guessed.

Jared clamped his jaw shut. Did he love Melissa? How could he love an illusion? He didn't even know which parts were her and which were the lie.

"And she loves you," Royce continued. He slowed for a stoplight, gearing the car down.

"I need a drink."

The woman was a damn fine illusion. If even half

of what he'd seen of her was real, it might be enough. Hell, it would be enough.

"What are you going to do?"

"Drink," said Jared.

Royce laughed. "Since you're not denying it and since you're even *considering* her, I'd say you absolutely need a drink. You've got it very bad, big brother."

"Why *her?*"

"It doesn't matter why her. It's done."

"Nothing's done." Jared certainly hadn't made any decisions. He was barely wrapping his head around falling for Melissa.

"You forget, I watched you watch her," said Royce. "You were never letting her go to Seattle."

"She never *was* going to Seattle. It was all a lie."

Royce shook his head and laughed. He glanced in the rearview mirror. Then he spun the steering wheel, yanked the hand brake and pivoted the car in a sharp u-turn.

"What are you doing?" Jared stabilized himself with the armrest.

"You *do* need a drink." Royce screeched to a stop in front of the Hilliard House tavern's valet parking. "If only to come to terms with the rest of your life."

Melissa should have realized her brother Caleb would call in reinforcements. She'd found herself at his house Saturday morning, looking for emotional support. Caleb was the most sympathetic of her brothers, and she'd really needed a shoulder to cry on.

Within an hour, Ben and Sheila had arrived, their

baby and two-year-old in tow. Then Eddy showed up, without the new girlfriend, demonstrating how seriously he was taking the situation. He was quick to envelop Melissa in a protective hug, and she had to battle a fresh round of tears.

Soon all her siblings and her nieces and nephews filled Caleb's big house with love and support. The jumble of their conversations and chaos of the children provided a buffer between Melissa and her raw emotions.

She'd told herself she couldn't be in love with Jared. Maybe it was infatuation. Maybe it was lust. She hadn't known him long enough for it to be real love.

But then she'd remember his voice, his smile, his jokes, his passion and the way she'd felt in his arms. What if it *was* real love? How was she going to get over it?

She swallowed, smiling as one of her nephews handed her a sticky wooden block, forcing her thoughts to the present.

The doors and windows of Caleb's house were wide open to the afternoon breeze. Some of her brothers were shooting hoops in the driveway while Adam cranked up the grill on the back deck and distributed bottles of imported beer. His wife, Renee, was calling out orders from the kitchen.

Melissa and her sister-in-law Sheila were corralling toddlers on the living-room floor, amid a jumble of blocks, action figures and miniature cars.

"Mellie?" Caleb's voice interrupted the game.

Melissa glanced up.

Her brother's brow was furrowed with concern, and she quickly saw the reason why.

Jared stood in the foyer, his suit and tie contrasting with the casual T-shirt and jeans Caleb wore.

She scrambled to her feet, drinking in his appearance, wishing she wasn't so pathetically glad to see him as she crammed her messy hair behind her ears. She hoped her eyes weren't red. She hoped he couldn't read how lonely she'd been the past few days. She'd fallen asleep each night with his image in her mind, longing to feel his strong arms wrapped around her.

She'd second-guessed herself a million times. What if she'd come clean right off? What if she'd told him who she was? Maybe he'd have thrown her off the ranch. But maybe he'd have given her an interview. And maybe, just maybe, they'd have had a chance to get to know each other without a lie between them.

She'd tried not to love him. She really had. But it was a hopeless proposition. And seeing him again told her that she'd be weeks, months, maybe even years getting over her feelings.

She heard a rustle from the kitchen and turned to see the rest of her brothers file in. They moved behind her, and Caleb joined them. As if it was choreographed, their muscular arms crossed over their chests and they pinned their gazes on Jared.

To his credit, Jared looked levelly back. "I see you didn't lie about your brothers."

The five Warner men straightened their spines and squared their shoulders. The toddlers' coos and burbles were at odds with the tension in the room.

"How did you find me?" Melissa managed to ask, searching Jared's expression, trying to figure out what reason he could possibly have for tracking her down. Had he somehow read an advance copy of the article? Had he hated it? Did he want her to change it?

"Your personnel file," Jared surprised her by answering. "Caleb is your emergency contact."

"How did you—"

"You're not fired, Melissa." He took a step forward. "I want you to know that up front."

She felt her brothers close ranks behind her.

"Oh, yes, I am," she responded, struggling to keep her voice from shaking. Seth had been crystal clear on that point.

Jared shook his head. "Ryder International bought *Windy City Bizz*. Nobody is firing you for anything."

Melissa peered at him, trying to make sense of his words.

"It was the best way I could think of to kill the story," he explained.

The babies played on in the background, while Renee and Sheila moved in beside their husbands.

Melissa subconsciously moved closer to Jared. "You bought the *Bizz?*"

"Yes."

That was insane.

"You paid, what? Thousands? Hundreds of thousands of dollars to keep my story out of the press?"

"I hadn't read the story when I bought the magazine." He offered a wry half smile. "Had I known it was so innocuous..."

"I did try to tell you," she pointed out.

"I know." His expression softened, and he moved closer still. "But you knew..." He glanced around at her family members, then peered at her to make sure she understood his code. "You know?"

She did, and she nodded. "I never would have used it."

"You lied. And I couldn't tell—"

"I am so sorry." She wished she could start over. If there was one minute in her life she could do over, it would be the first time they met. She'd tell Jared she was a reporter up front and let him do whatever he would do.

"Mellie." Caleb's arm went around her. "You don't have to apologize again."

"Agreed," said Jared, meeting Caleb's eyes, squaring his own shoulders. "It's my turn to apologize. I lied to her, too."

Caleb tensed, but Jared stepped forward, anyway, clasping his hands over Melissa's. His hands were warm and strong, sending sensory memories tingling along her spine.

His expression softened again, and his voice went lower. "I lied to you when I said I never wanted to see you again."

Melissa felt a faint flicker of hope. But she instantly squelched it. She was going down a dangerous road, erasing any gains she'd made since that horrible night at the Ritz-Carlton.

"I do want to see you again," Jared continued, and

she was forced to redouble her effort at dampening her hope. "All the time. Every day from here on in."

Melissa wanted to run. She wanted to hide. Her brain couldn't comprehend that he might be serious.

"Excuse me?" Sheila popped out from behind the men. "What are you saying to Melissa?"

Jared flicked an annoyed glance at Sheila, and Melissa could feel her brother Ben bristle.

"I'm saying," said Jared, a thread of steel coming into his voice, "I can propose to her here under, well, rather stressful circumstances."

His gaze went back to Melissa while her heart thudded powerfully in her chest. "Or we can go somewhere private, where I can do it properly."

Her mind scrambled in a freefall.

"I have a limo out front," Jared continued. "A table on the deck at the Bayside, a florist and photographer on standby, also—" he tapped the breast of his suit "—a ring. I also have a ring."

"Can we see it?" chirped Sheila.

Jared's attention never left Melissa. "Only if she says yes."

Melissa couldn't do anything but blink. Emotions that had been close to the surface for days threatened to erupt. This couldn't be happening. It must be some fevered hallucination.

She looked back at her family.

They were watching expectantly.

Could this be happening? Could it be real? If she'd had a free hand, she'd have pinched himself.

"Melissa?" Jared prompted.

"I think—" she nodded "—the restaurant is a good idea."

"Yeah?" A grin split his face.

"And the photographer." She assured herself it was all real. Jared had found her. And he wanted to be with her. "I have a feeling Stephanie will expect pictures."

Jared's grin widened.

Sheila spoke out. "But can we see the—"

Ben clapped a hand over her mouth.

It took her all of three seconds to escape. "Good grief. It's obvious she's going to say yes. They can reenact it later for the photographer."

Everyone stared openmouthed at Sheila.

"What?" she asked. "Come on, Renee. Back me up. We want to see the ring."

Adam's wife stepped forward. "I have to say, I'm with Sheila on this."

Melissa started to laugh. "Go ahead," she told Jared. She *was* planning to say yes.

"In a minute," he told her, stepping back to pull Melissa into the foyer, around the corner, beyond the view of her family.

He held her hand firmly, staring into her eyes. "I love you."

The world disappeared around them, and Melissa's chest filled with a warm shimmering glow. The worries lifted off her shoulders and the vestiges of pain evaporated from inside her.

"I love you, too," she breathed, touching his face, letting his essence seep through her fingertips and into her soul.

Jared sobered as he leaned in for a kiss. His lips touched hers and magic seem to saturate the atmosphere around them. It was a very long minute before he pulled back.

"We can reenact this part later for the camera," he whispered, reaching to his inside jacket pocket. "But will you marry me?" He flipped open the jewel case to reveal a stunning solitaire.

Melissa nodded. "Yes. Oh, yes." She couldn't imagine a more amazing future than one with Jared.

He slipped the ring onto her finger. Then he kissed her hand and whispered, "Go ahead and show it off."

Though her family was waiting, Jared was her world. She went up on tiptoe, hugging him tight, and he lifted her off the floor to spin her around.

Sheila squealed in the background, and suddenly the entire family was pouring into the foyer, admiring Melissa's engagement ring and welcoming Jared into the family.

*Rancher Ramsey Westmoreland's temporary cook
is way too attractive for his liking.
Little does he know Chloe Burton came to his ranch
with another agenda entirely....*

That man across the street had to be, without a doubt, the most handsome man she'd ever seen.

Chloe Burton's pulse beat rhythmically as he stopped to talk to another man in front of a feed store. He was tall, dark and every inch of sexy—from his Stetson to the well-worn leather boots on his feet. And from the way his jeans and Western shirt fit his broad muscular shoulders, it was quite obvious he had everything it took to separate the men from the boys. The combination was enough to corrupt any woman's mind and had her weakening even from a distance. Her body felt flushed. It was hot. Unsettled.

Over the past year the only male who had gotten her time and attention had been the e-mail. That was simply pathetic, especially since now she was practically drooling simply at the sight of a man. Even his stance—both hands in his jeans pockets, legs braced apart, was a pose she would carry to her dreams.

And he was smiling, evidently enjoying the conversation being exchanged. He had dimples, incredibly sexy dimples in not one but both cheeks.

"What are you staring at, Clo?"

Chloe nearly jumped. She'd forgotten she had a lunch date. She glanced over the table at her best friend from college, Lucia Conyers.

"Take a look at that man across the street in the blue shirt, Lucia. Will he not be perfect for Denver's first issue of *Simply Irresistible* or what?" Chloe asked with so much excitement she almost couldn't stand it.

She was the owner of *Simply Irresistible,* a magazine for today's up-and-coming woman. Their once-a-year Irresistible Man cover, which highlighted a man the magazine felt deserved the honor, had increased sales enough for Chloe to open a Denver office.

When Lucia didn't say anything but kept staring, Chloe's smile widened. "Well?"

Lucia glanced across the booth at her. "Since you asked, I'll tell you what I see. One of the Westmorelands—Ramsey Westmoreland. And yes, he'd be perfect for the cover, but he won't do it."

Chloe raised a brow. "He'd get paid for his services, of course."

Lucia laughed and shook her head. "Getting paid won't be the issue, Clo—Ramsey is one of the wealthiest sheep ranchers in this part of Colorado. But everyone knows what a private person he is. Trust me—he won't do it."

Chloe couldn't help but smile. The man was the epitome of what she was looking for in a magazine cover and she was determined that whatever it took, he would be it.

"Umm, I don't like that look on your face, Chloe. I've seen it before and know exactly what it means."

She watched as Ramsey Westmoreland entered the store with a swagger that made her almost breathless. She *would* be seeing him again.

Look for Silhouette Desire's
HOT WESTMORELAND NIGHTS
by Brenda Jackson,
available March 9 wherever books are sold.

Devastating, dark-hearted and...
looking for brides.

Look for

BOUGHT:
DESTITUTE YET DEFIANT
by *Sarah Morgan*
#2902

From the lowliest slums to Millionaire's Row...
these men have everything now but their brides—
and they'll settle for nothing less than the best!

Available March 2010
from Harlequin Presents!

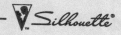

SPECIAL EDITION

FROM *USA TODAY* BESTSELLING AUTHOR
CHRISTINE RIMMER

A BRIDE FOR
JERICHO BRAVO

Marnie Jones had long ago buried her wild-child
impulses and opted to be "safe," romantically
speaking. But one look at born rebel Jericho Bravo
and she began to wonder if her thrill-seeking side
was about to be revived. Because if ever there was
a man worth taking a chance on, there he was,
right within her grasp....

*Available in March
wherever books are sold.*

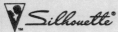

ROMANTIC SUSPENSE

Sparked by Danger, Fueled by Passion.

Introducing a brand-new miniseries
Lawmen of Black Rock

Peyton Wilkerson's life shatters when her
four-month-old daughter, Lilly, vanishes.
But handsome sheriff Tom Grayson is
determined to put the pieces together and
reunite her with her baby. Will Tom be able
to protect Peyton and Lilly while fighting
his own growing feelings?

Find out in

His Case, Her Baby

by

CARLA CASSIDY

Available in March wherever books are sold

Visit Silhouette Books at www.eHarlequin.com

SRS27670

REQUEST YOUR FREE BOOKS!

2 FREE NOVELS
PLUS 2
FREE GIFTS!

Silhouette

Desire®

Passionate, Powerful, Provocative!

Silhouette *Desire*

THE WESTMORELANDS

NEW YORK TIMES
bestselling author

BRENDA JACKSON

HOT WESTMORELAND NIGHTS

Ramsey Westmoreland knew better than to lust after the hired help. But Chloe, the new cook, was just so delectable. Though their affair was growing steamier, Chloe's motives became suspicious. And when he learned Chloe was carrying his child this Westmoreland Rancher had to choose between pride or duty.

Available March 2010 wherever books are sold.

Always Powerful, Passionate and Provocative.